To fin

Call o
Snow Dolphin

A Spirited Pacific Spree

You can do anything!

Tess Burrows

Tess Burrows

Lightning Books

Praise for 'Call of the Snow Dolphin'

'Utterly absorbing! An emotional roller coaster of an adventure. You won't want to miss it!'
Annie Pritchard
Counsellor and runner

'A fun story that makes me want to go adventuring. I can relate to the hero, Kai, and his friends going through all the dramas, both in the dreams and the physical reality'
Evelyn
Age 12

'An absolutely charming tale of resilience, courage, persistence and wisdom! *Call of the Snow Dolphin* features a diverse range of settings and a line-up of fascinating international characters. It is full of intrigue and wonder.

Kai's journey is ultimately centred on love and the book's message is a serious environmentalist and compassionate one. Yet the story is told vividly, with humour, and with hope at its core.

As an English teacher I will be wholeheartedly recommending this book to my students – though I must say I was also gripped by it as an adult reader!'
Emma Silverthorn
Educator and author

'"When human thoughts become peaceful, then violence on earth will stop," says the Snow Dolphin. This important book is a crucial message, cleverly woven together for humankind. Wisdom, humour and magic shine from every page'

Lis Moss

Teacher and subtle-energy therapist

'A wonderful teenage fantasy adventure, interwoven with mysticism and the important message of listening to Gaia in our fight to halt climate change'

Julia Lee

Reiki and animal healer

'This story brings real-life magic to the race that must be won'

Miles Barrington-Ward

Accountant and snow enthusiast

'Tess Burrows does it again! Her unique voice rings true across the universe and literary world alike, setting her apart. Her wholesome book is full of hope and messages for today's younger generations and those to come. Her characterisation is relatable and her fantastical creation of the snow dolphin is original and captivating. This is an absolute must-read - for all ages'

Lorraine Kennedy

Teacher and mother of 13-year-olds

Published in 2024
by Lightning Books Ltd
Imprint of Eye Books Ltd
29A Barrow Street
Much Wenlock
Shropshire
TF13 6EN

www.lightning-books.com

Illustrations by Elsie Burrows
Cover by Prem Shashi
Dolphin border: Bessie Burrows
Model for running boy: Bodhi Burrows

British Library Cataloguing in Publication Data
A catalogue record for this book is available from the British Library.

ISBN: 9781785634048

With love
for my grandson Atticus
and the children of our Earth.
That they may live the dream...

And thank you to the dolphins!

Invitation from the Snow Dolphin

Dear Reader,

How's your sonar? Can you feel beyond your five main senses? Like dolphins or, best of all, like snow dolphins.

Want to know more?

Once upon a time, there were snow dolphins who lived high on the volcanos of Hawaii, in the snow fields that grew in the winter chills and softened in the summer sun.

They had emerged with fiery earth-blood, erupting onto this beautiful land. Then frozen sky water came, forming the perfect matrix for their home. There, they were given wisdom, and charged with the task of holding peace, as guardians of the world.

They were never given bodies in the vibration of the physical like their brothers and sisters in the seas, who were the keepers of the wisdom. Instead they were nurtured by the natural magic in the crystals of the pure mountain ice. And held in the clouds of time and space, where they could journey through the dreams of those that walk the earth, swim the seas and fly the skies.

In this way they were the voice of the sea dolphins, whispering their wisdom to other beings to help hold the world in balance.

But one day things changed. The land, the seas and the skies started to warm. And the ice crystals began to melt away, becoming irregular and uncertain. It was no longer possible for the crystals to sustain a whole pod of snow dolphins.

One by one they left... Until...now... only one remains...

I am the last of the snow dolphins. I call to you; to feel on your sonar, the beauty of dolphin magic; to be the hero of your own life.

And invite you to listen to my dream-story – the tale of a young human...

THE SNOW DOLPHIN

1
Chosen

He was chosen, out of all the kids in the whole world – chosen by the only creature with a brain bigger and more complex than a human.

Yikes!

A creature who has been around on this Earth for millions of years and, legend tells, holds knowledge for humanity.

Wow!

Kai considered his life to be normal before speaking with the dolphin.

There was the usual school day in a sleepy harbour town in south-west England, fun walking home with friends, though always, "Sorry, I can't come to the beach, Mum's not well," which they thankfully understood.

Then that wonderful moment of walking in the door of the little cottage and being greeted enthusiastically by Bandit the dog, whose injured hind leg sent him round in circles when he wagged his tail hard. Kai would laugh and bury his face in the dog's warm fur and tell him, "I'll rush through the chores, then we'll go out."

Together they'd make Mum a cup of tea and tidy up after her day struggling from a wheelchair. Then do the washing and cook the dinner and finally take Bandit out to the headland, overlooking an ever-changing sea, and run in sheer delight, kicking a football together.

Whoopee!

Kai often thought how nice it would be to have a brother or sister to share everything with, but he was grateful to have Bandit.

Even more so as Dad had no time for him. "Get

out from under me feet!" he'd say, tolerating Kai so long as he did his chores. Kai didn't understand why Dad never seemed to care about his family – only about making money at the plastic bag factory where he worked. It made him sad.

Anyway there was always homework to think about, generally hurried through before falling asleep, curled up on a box-bed in a tiny attic room. Boy with dog and soft-toy animal from babyhood cuddled together.

He was content enough. It was the life he knew, hard as it was caring for Mum and doing the chores, but safe and settled.

The best things in life often sneak up on us unannounced. So it was with Kai, who had no idea that the day of the school trip to the island nature reserve was to be so momentous. It was certainly the most eagerly anticipated outing of the school programme. All his year group had signed up for it.

Mum had sent money out of her savings to pay for the boat for him to go. She was excited for him, and all smiles that day, which was rare. He couldn't deny her that pleasure by not going. Trouble was, he knew he'd be sea-sick.

And worse, he was scared. He was frightened of the sea. For as long as he could remember he'd shake with fear at the thought of swimming. It was quite irrational, but his heart would start beating faster and his mouth would go dry.

Stupid or what?

He never told anyone. How could he? Mum had enough worries. Dad didn't care. And his friends... Well, it just seemed too silly, especially when they were so excited at heading into the waves.

A technique had somehow come about to get out of it. When the class was having surfing lessons, he'd say to the teacher, "Please can I run instead?" And he'd be sent to run along the beach until the lesson was over. He'd always head for the sand dunes and revel in the wonderful free feeling of bounding up and sliding down the steep loose slopes, just him and the grasses and the wind. He'd never tire of it. Everyone thought it was the running he loved.

Oops!

At least he had long legs which meant he ran effortlessly without becoming tired. But they made him tall – head and shoulders above his friends, which he found embarrassing. He'd try and look shorter by bending his head whenever he could, but Dad would shout at him, "Stand up properly, lad! Don't slouch!"

As if that wasn't enough, his forehead was a funny shape. It just seemed to stick out too much. He'd been self-conscious about it ever since he'd had a shoving fight with a boy at school who'd called him a freak. It made him feel insecure. Why couldn't he be more like everyone else?

It was tough.

"C'mon mate, the boat's leaving," his friend Luke urged, pulling at his shirt sleeve. Luke was bossy with a mane of ginger hair. Together they looked like a lion and a tall giraffe, according to their spunky blond friend Daniella. But, even though Kai towered above his friends in height, being with them gave him confidence.

He followed them onto the gangplank over to the black and white ferry, with masts waving coloured flags, and school kids all excited. It sprang up and down as he took a deep breath, muttering, "I don't like this." Then as the deck rocked and the engine thrummed, he went down into the cabin area, pretending he wasn't on the ocean with all that depth of water beneath him.

Sitting on a bench, he tried to ignore the tipping land horizon disappearing through the window. But then it turned to the swell of grey-green sea, and the smell of the oily engine became overpowering. He rushed up the wooden stairs, pushed his way through milling bodies, and thrust his head over the edge, vomiting violently – like he'd just eaten four pizzas in a row! The cold wind on his face did nothing to help his churning stomach, but it did clear away all the other kids, squealing "Ugh!" as the wind blew its contents back onto the boat.

Yuk!

He'd never felt so miserable in all his life, even when Dad shouted at Mum.

He crawled to a tarpaulin at the front of the boat from where he could hide at the same time as carry on vomiting. Even the terror of looking down at the waves crashing and soaking him in spray paled to insignificance as he no longer cared what happened.

He flopped head down on the wood right at the edge and didn't even bother to wipe embarrassing tears away.

That was when it happened.

Someone called his name.

"Kai!"

It hit him in the middle of his forehead. "Kai! We're here now... Be ready for adventure."

There was whistling among the splashing of the waves. And beneath his gaze he saw a dark-grey streamlined shape dancing over the bow-wave.

Dolphin!

A whoosh of elation rushed through him, giving him the energy to reach out with a hand. As he did so there was a bolt of shiny mass which threw itself at him, brushing his finger-tips. It felt smooth like rubber. He'd been touched by a dolphin!

"Hello," he was able to gasp as he looked into an eye as deep as an ocean, as wide as a sky.

Then suddenly there were many dolphins, bringing an orchestra of clicks, whistles and squeaks, breaching again and again over the bow wave, keeping up with the boat, jumping seemingly in sheer delight. And he heard unmistakably through his forehead, "The prophecy of the ancients..." followed by the trilling words of their chorus, "There will come a boy..."

The sunlight caught rainbow sparkles among the spray.

Then the dolphins were gone.

Kai didn't know it then, but his life would never be the same again.

2
The Unbreakable Promise

His friends, Luke and Daniella, found him a little later. "We've been searching for you, Kai. Are you okay?" The three of them had grown up playing football together in their home street and always looked out for each other.

"Dolphins!" he beamed. "I've been talking with dolphins," sickness and misery eclipsed by excitement.

"No way!"

"Why didn't we see them?"

"Hey Mr Jellyman," Daniella called to their class tutor, "Kai's seen dolphins!"

Mr Jellyman staggered over, holding tight onto the railing. His build was of the large and round variety which was not ideal for sea voyages, but the kids liked him as he always took time to listen to what they had to say.

"Dolphins! Unique in their intelligence, cooperation and playfulness...and they even show compassion. Wonderful!" he enthused. "They are one of the most important and fascinating animals on the planet." He talked to the class about Kai's sighting for the rest of the journey and all day as they walked around the island, spotting grey seals and rare sea birds. And even on the way back to the mainland. But there were no more dolphins to be seen. It made Kai feel special.

That evening Mum was sitting up having a rare hour of feeling okay, so he went on about it. "It was so amazing, like the dolphin only wanted to speak to me!"

"Probably because you've always cuddled your soft-toy dolphin in bed," Mum said. "Ever since you were a baby and Granny gave Phinny to you. So you're in tune with dolphins."

"Hmm..." Kai had never really thought about

Phinny being a dolphin. He was always just that comforting blankety friend who was there for him when life was tough and who somehow made things okay.

It reminded him that Phinny was the one thing that connected him to Granny. This gave him a warm loving feeling. And a surprising sense of belonging. He tried to think what it was she had said to him about Phinny as she lay on the hospital bed just before she died, but he couldn't. All he could remember was that desperate sense of pain and loneliness as she said, "I'm sorry I won't be around any more, Kai dear. Please look after Mum for me."

And he remembered his, "I will. I promise," through fast-falling tears.

Even now, five years on, Kai felt the lump in his throat.

Dad marched in then. "So you've been 'aving a day off, 'ave you, lad? Waste of time an' money!"

"We learnt a lot about wildlife today, Dad."

"Should've been workin' at school for exams if you ask me."

"It's part of the curriculum to study an island close to nature without interference from humans." Kai spoke carefully, always mindful not to upset his dad. He was a big man, given to angry outbursts, and Kai had been on the receiving end of the back of his hand more times than he cared to think about. Mostly, though, he wanted to protect his mum, who was in no position to defend herself from her wheelchair.

"C'mon Bandit – homework to do." He rushed up to his room trying not to hear Dad's angry words, "I've told you we can't afford extra school trips. We're not made of money!"

Sleep was difficult to settle into that night. Kai's thoughts were going round and round. What was the adventure that dolphin was talking about? And how come he heard what the dolphins were saying, anyway? And what did this prophecy have to do with him?

3
The First Dream

"Kai!" Someone's speaking his name.

The warm smooth voice continues, "We're here now. Be ready for adventure."

It floats over him, bringing a peaceful sense that everything's as it should be. And he smiles to himself, knowing he's hearing in the middle of his forehead and not his ears.

"You can open your eyes. It's okay."

His eyelids are stuck tight together as though he'd really rather not be dreaming.

"Turnin' turtles! Go on!"

He tries to force them apart by stretching his face upwards and shaking his head. Suddenly they flick open. And he sees, right in front of him a long beak that looks like a grey wellyboot with teeth jutting out. He stares in shocked silence, unbelieving…

"I actually sleep with one eye open. You should try. It's supercool!" the friendly voice continues. "That way you don't miss out on anything." There's a sort of clicking giggle accompanied by bubbles that set off upwards, sparkling in light.

Kai stares at them. And senses the heavy liquid all around. Then it dawns on him… He's underwater! "Help!" he gasps. "I can't do water! I'm scared!" A tight band of panic grips him around his chest. He splutters. His heart starts beating faster and faster. All he can think is; I'm going to drown! I'm going to die! He desperately starts thrashing with arms and legs.

That's when a forceful shove from underneath catapults him upwards, with his lungs feeling like they'll explode. And suddenly he's rushing out of the water, momentarily flying, then wham! splashing down on the surface, gurgling under again, until he pops up like toast. Then at last he knows he can breathe air and gulps mouthfuls gratefully.

Phew!

He's sure he can hear those clicking giggles again. Looking round, he's on the surface of a gently rolling dream-blue sea. And there're dolphins everywhere. Some jumping, some diving, some just swimming around, dark grey fins piercing the swell, but all playing and having fun.

"It's okay, Kai. It's supercool," the voice softly soothes beside him. And he stares at the grey wellyboot with long sleek torpedo body, two flippers working alongside over a white tummy. There's a long upturned beak, like a permanent smile complete with dimples, surely laughing, not so much at him but just in delight. The animal looks at him with eyes that are deep and loving and somehow familiar. Kai relaxes.

"You're a dolphin!"

"Of course I'm a dolphin. What d'you think I am? A supercharged wellyboot?" That clicking giggle again.

"Well, actually…"

"Dumpin' dogfish! Never mind. Let me introduce myself." There's a startling whistle. "I'm your dolphin dream guide. And these," he waves a flipper at the antics that are going on all around them, "are my brothers and sisters."

"That's an awful lot of brothers and sisters."

"Yes, Kai... It's a big family."

How nice to have such a large family, Kai thinks, wondering, 'how did he know my name, anyway?'

"Your name is part of the energy signature you give off."

"It is? But how did you know I was wondering how you knew my name?"

"Turnin' turtles! I can hear your thoughts," the dolphin says.

"You can?"

"And I can see your heart-light."

"You can?" This is most confusing, Kai thinks.

Then the dolphin makes it worse by saying, "I've been trying to get your attention for a while."

"You have?"

"Managed it with the dolphins on the boat today, didn't I?"

Just as Kai is working out what's going on there's a loud whacking down of a tail on the water surface – a kerploosh – and shouts of "Dive now!"

Kai woke with a start. He was clutching his soft-toy dolphin tightly. Bandit was asleep on his feet. He looked up at his skylight window and saw stars twinkling through the usual mucky glass that he always meant to clean. It'd been a dream! Oh, dratbag! How disappointing! There'd been something so real about the encounter.

He gently shifted Bandit and, grabbing a t-shirt, wiped the dirt from the window so he could see the stars more clearly. There were patterns that he knew, almost like friends, though he didn't know their names. And one really bright star that always intrigued him. He loved to take in the magic of the universe up there. Feel the hugeness. And the unknownness.

He hadn't remembered a dream for quite a few days. So, why now, after the boat trip today? And surely this one was telling him something important?

Somehow he couldn't shake off the feeling that it'd been more than a dream.

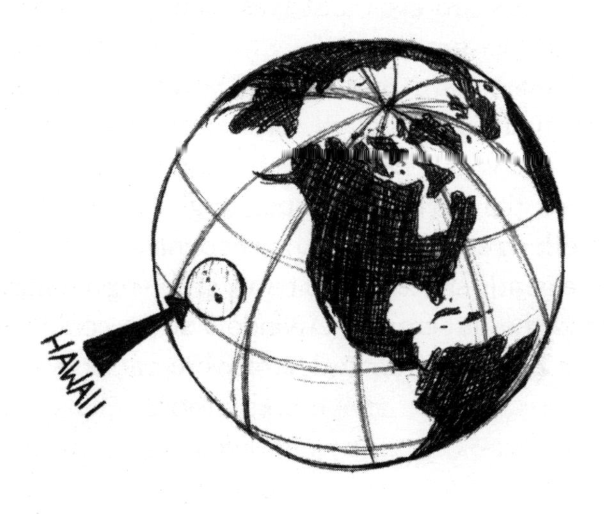

4
The Amazing Race

The next day at school Mr Jellyman asked everyone to stand up and do a two-minute talk about their experience on the island. It was tougher than it sounded to speak for that long. Luke chatted about seeing cool puffins giving each other feathers and tumbling down cliffs. Daniella spoke about rats, banned on the island 'cos of eating sea-bird eggs, but was sure a rat had run off with her sandwich!

When it came to Kai's turn he shyly stood up, trying to be as un-tall as possible, fiddling with his desk, and said, "Well, I don't know really, but..."

"Yes, Kai?" prompted Mr Jellyman.

"...It made me think we should take care of all the beautiful animals. So that's what I'm going to do... Protect nature. And..." He paused, "I'm going to look after the dolphins." He sat down, suddenly aware that everyone was looking at him in silence, and wished he could disappear into the floor.

"Well done, Kai," said Mr Jellyman, smashing his fist down on the table so enthusiastically that his bottom wiggled, making everyone laugh, which covered Kai's embarrassment. As the end-of-lesson bell rang he added, "And please stay for a minute. There's something I want to ask you."

When they were alone, he began, "The school's been invited to enter a candidate for a running race to highlight the Natural World Crisis. The headmistress said we didn't have any runners, but I put forward your name, reminding her that you'd had the endurance to win that inter-schools cross-country match for us – though you didn't even want to take part. She agreed, if you were happy about it. I know you run quite a bit during surfing lessons. What d'you think?"

"No, no! I only do that... My dad would never let me."

"All costs paid. And there's very substantial prize money."

Kai was busy shaking his head, but then for some reason he remembered his promise to Granny about looking after Mum. And he thought: if I can win some money, then Mum can have that operation that's too rare and expensive for the health service. It'll help her body work better and she can go back to work, which she badly wants to do, and it'll vastly improve her life.

Mr Jellyman continued. "A couple of sentences is needed to show what the candidate's purpose of life is, so I think what you just said to the class will work very well... Hmm... Yes indeed, I think we can use that... They're looking for thirteen-year-olds with good English, yes...but also an unusual sensitivity to nature...and I'm sure you have something special with dolphins... So, how about we put your name down anyway? I think the chances of being picked out of the whole country are very slim – only two kids from each continent – but of course you've got to be, 'in it to win it'. And it seems to be more about attitude than being able to run."

Kai found himself nodding.

"Don't you want to know where it is?" Mr Jellyman asked.

Kai raised his eyes to those of Mr Jellyman, which were sparkling with expectation.

"This amazing race is to run up the world's tallest mountain…in Hawaii…in the middle of the Pacific Ocean!"

"Oh, wow!… But isn't Everest the tallest mountain?"

"No. This one – White Mountain – is a volcano which starts nearly 6,000 metres below the ocean and rises 4,207 metres above, making it taller than Everest, which is only 8,848!"

"That's so cool!" Kai was fascinated. He couldn't share Mr Jellyman's excitement, as he knew he'd never be picked, but it was amazing to have his tutor express such confidence in him. And even just considering it… Well, that was beyond his wildest dreams. Wow! And in just one minute, somehow his personal world had been expanded to include the whole planet! And this woke something deep inside him that wanted more from life.

5

Dolphin Dream Guide

That night Kai lay in bed, Bandit at his feet, wondering what secrets the Pacific Ocean might hold for him... As a daring explorer, never sea-sick...sailing into the setting sun...on a raft of trunks of trees bound by vines, old shirt for a sail... guided by playing dolphins...to an island where dancers on a white-sandy beach were swaying rhythmically with the palm trees...

He wasn't in the least surprised when he felt water all around... And a wellyboot-sort-of presence bobbing beside him, with flippers flapping...

"Hi Kai. We're here now. Be ready for adventure."

"Oh, hi Dolphin Dream Guide. What're ya doing?"

"Spy-hopping."

"What's spy-hopping?"

"It's working hard to stay vertical with my head above the water, to communicate with a human boy who doesn't like getting his hair wet."

Kai tries to shove him playfully, though not quickly enough. The dolphin glides effortlessly away with a huge grin. But Kai is more interested in finding some answers to puzzling things. "So if you're my dream guide, where do you live when you're not spy-hopping?"

"I inhabit your soft-toy dolphin."

"Phinny! Really?"

"Yup... Why not?"

"Well, I've known Phinny all my life and he's never

had anyone live in him before."

"Turnin' turtles! Life evolves."

"I guess so."

"Anyway, the Snow Dolphin – she's my boss who speaks for the dolphins – offered me this assignment because I'm experienced at inhabiting soft-toy bodies. In fact, I'm unique. I was a penguin once. But that's another story..."

"Oh!"

"It means I can be close to you when you're asleep."

"Ah!"

"And look after you."

"Sort of like a guardian angel?"

"Dumpin' dogfish! Not sure I'd go that far..."

"So, I'd better call you Phinny."

"Well, that name's a bit soppy isn't it? I was hoping for something a bit more warrior-like... that makes me feel important." He pulls himself up tall in his skin and looks around, hoping there're no dolphins listening, aware of his ego, Degbert – that snooty part of him who thinks it knows all the answers.

"Mum said once that Phinny's proper name is Phinneas. That's a bit grander."

There's a definite puffing out of the chest of the dolphin. "Supercool! Better than the names I've had in previous assignments... I like it."

"On the other hand I think I prefer Wellyboot," says Kai, enjoying himself now. Though he isn't prepared when Phinneas stops spy-hopping and splashes down hard on the water with his flippers, soaking them both, then wrestling the boy under the water, rolling over and over until they finally come up laughing and spluttering.

"Okay Phinn. You win!" Kai shouts.

"Supercool Phinn is in!" comes the shout back. "And we're going to have a lot of fun in your dreams."

Kai smiles. "I can't believe my boy body just went underwater so happily."

"Turnin' turtles! You have an expert dream guide!"

"Yikes!"

"And the exciting thing is that in your dreams, I, Phinneas, have a dolphin body."

"How does that work?"

"Because you're dreaming me."

"Ah, I guess..."

"You'll soon get the hang of it..." Phinn circles round Kai, enjoying creating a whirlpool. "C'mon. I want to show you how to dive for pebbles."

"Wait! Tell me. Are you able to be around when I'm awake?"

"Only on special occasions when the Snow Dolphin allows me to take on the body of a physical dolphin, like with the boat to the island... That was supercool! But mostly we have to communicate through your soft-toy Phinny when you're asleep."

"But..." Kai worries thoughtfully, "what happens when I can't remember my dreams. Half the time I nearly remember them when I wake up, and then they disappear."

"You'll remember the important bits," Phinn says. "And dumpin' dogfish! The more you practise the better you'll get, until..."

6
A Bandit Friend

Kai felt a lump on his chest and a long smooth tongue licking his face.

He pushed Bandit off, saying crossly, "Oy! Please don't wake me up when I'm having important dreams."

Bandit looked put out.

"I'm sorry...of course I love you... Come here."

He fondled the dog's ears, thinking over the dream conversation. "Maybe we can get you into the dreams too..."

It was over two weeks before Kai was drawn aside by Mr Jellyman again. He'd been playing football on the pitches and running as hard as he could, just in case... So he was pleased to see Mr Jellyman watching – the only one who understood. He hadn't dared tell anyone else about the race. It was their secret.

"Kai, bad news I'm afraid," said Mr Jellyman gently. "We were notified today by the race authorities that the European contestants have been chosen – a girl from Ireland who has a great affinity with plants, and a boy from Finland who's won every race going and is a staunch activist for climate change. But your application was very favourably received. They liked your initiative and potential. I did write a very good report for you."

"Thank you, Mr Jellyman," said Kai, biting his lip. His hopes dashed into fragments at his feet. He'd never had an opportunity to go beyond the town and do something that made a difference. It seemed that it would always be like that.

Walking home with Luke and Daniella he hung his head and was silent. "Whats up?" they asked repeatedly. He just shrugged, "Nothing," and shot off to do his chores, trying hard not to cry.

That night Kai buried his face in Bandit's soft fur and let the misery out, sniffing, "I'll never be able to make something of myself…or do anything worthwhile… I'm no good…"

Dratbag!

The dog tried to cheer him up by lying as close as he possibly could to his boy – protector and playmate.

"I feel so much better with you here. Thank you."

And so it happened that he went to sleep holding Bandit on his mind.

7
Not-so-smelly Dogpoo

They're all running across the waves. Phinn the dolphin leading them, Kai the boy marvelling at their swift motion, and Bandit the dog moving smoothly without his hind leg wobble. All jumping and diving in fun, with starlight reflecting off the spray of dark seas... On and on, twisting this way and that, as ragged coastlines pass by. And now flying, seeing the world move faster, far below. It feels to Kai like the journey is never-ending.

"Where are we going?" he asks.

"You'll see," says Phinn, with a mysterious grin. "Dumpin' dogfish! Keep up!"

At last they slow and a coastal town comes into view beneath them. Lines of lamp posts send their light out through a ghostly mist, showing steep-roofed houses along streets of white.

"It's snow!" shouts Kai, excitedly. He floats down, hoping to see soft fluffy stuff, but is disappointed to find slippery icy slush. At least he doesn't feel cold. There are advantages in being in a dream body.

It's very early morning, so nobody's about. All is quiet.

"We need to wait," Phinn says, hovering in front of a pale green house with a light in one window.

It's quite dark still. There's only a faint glimmer of dawn with grey sleety rain.

They wait.

Kai practises cool dream somersaults in the air. After some concentration, he works out the secret is to lift his arms up and pull down quickly while curling and rolling his body... He wonders if the movement will work the same underwater.

Phinn has a play in the pond across the road and herds a few surprised ducks, cracking through thin ice.

And Bandit does what dogs do best. He enjoys sniffing around and watering all the lamp posts, finishing off with a nice fat poo on the pavement.

"Hey, you two," calls Phinn. "Come and watch..."

A boy comes out of the house. He looks athletic and strong as he pulls up the hood on his red jacket and blows on his hands. He checks his watch and starts running down the street, softly on his feet, almost flowing, faster and faster, steadily focusing on his run. Mist swirls in and out The rest of the houses are silent and without lights. Still asleep. All quiet.

Until an alarm bell rings.

"Oh, dratbag!" Kai had set his alarm to wake him up early so he could finish his homework.

"That was fun being in the dream, Bandit, wasn't it?" he said, vigorously stroking the dog's back and massaging his wobbly hind leg. "It was just beginning to get interesting. No idea what it was all about... Where do you think we were?"

The dog was just happy that the boy was happy.

Later that day, Kai was busy practising air somersaults in his mind during assembly, so it was a while before he noticed that Mr Jellyman was looking agitated. Normally the teachers sat stiffly while the headmistress gave out notices. But Mr Jellyman was shifting around on his bottom and twitching bits of his beard. And every now and again he would look at Kai, who began to be intrigued by this behaviour. What was going on? Was he in trouble? Maybe he'd been spotted letting those mice go free out of the cages – the ones meant for dissecting in science. He'd been so sure nobody was watching.

"Kai. See me afterwards, please," Mr Jellyman said as they all filed out of the hall. Oh, dratbag! He couldn't get out of it.

"Kai, I need to come and speak with your parents tonight," said Mr Jellyman outside, looking serious.

"But Mr Jellyman, my father won't like it..."

"It's urgent, Kai. I'll be at your house at eight o'clock."

There was nothing he could do about it. But whatever could he tell Dad? Best keep it a surprise.

Somehow he managed to warn Mum, rush through his chores, take Bandit out and be waiting nervously in the sitting room, tucking a blanket around Mum in her wheelchair, by the time there was a knock on the door at eight o'clock.

"Don't want no visitors this time of night," Dad said, annoyed.

"I'll get it, Dad." Kai rushed up to open the door, wishing he could disappear under the carpet, and ushered a clean and tidy Mr Jellyman in.

"Ah, Mr and Mrs Duckworth. I'm Kai's class tutor. So sorry to disturb you at this time but it's important I talk with you about your son."

"What's 'e done now?... Always knew 'e was up to no good, that—"

"No, no, it's all good, I assure you... You must be very proud of him."

There was an awkward silence during which Kai grabbed Mum's hand. She squeezed it reassuringly.

"Out with it, man. What is it?" Dad grumbled.

"Well...an opportunity has come up...for Kai to represent the school...and Europe actually... in a running race. It's all to highlight the Natural World Crisis. The race authorities picked a boy in Finland. But he's had an unfortunate accident – it appears he was out running and slipped on some dogpoo and broke his leg. So it means they have to fill his place urgently... The training starts next week in Hawaii. And...and basically...they would like your son to go."

Kai's mouth dropped open. His eyes widened in surprise, then excitement, and then realisation. His hand went to his mouth.

Mum smiled.

Dad appeared stunned. "Oh, good God!... But, but my son can't run and don't know nothing 'bout any Natural World Crisis, and it's certainly out of the question as we can't afford it."

"All expenses paid," said Mr Jellyman firmly.

Dad was shaking his head.

Kai got up and went over to Dad and knelt at his feet pleadingly – something he'd never done before, "Please, Dad... I can do it. I know I can!"

Dad pushed him away.

"The school thinks it's a good idea and will support him all the way," Mr Jellyman added.

"No... It's not possible. We need 'im 'ere to look after 'is mother," Dad insisted. Then rose to his feet and showed Mr Jellyman the door. "I think you should go now, man... You've caused enough problems for one day."

Kai glanced desperately at Mum, slumped in her wheelchair with a how-ever-can-we-sort-this look on her face.

The door banged loudly behind Mr Jellyman, slamming shut on all Kai's dreams.

8
In Trouble with the Boss

Kai couldn't wait to get to bed. He wanted to talk with Phinn. He realised he was already remembering his dreams better, not only when woken up suddenly, but also by focusing on them first thing, as he woke up. He was developing a habit. Even better he saw he had some control – like thinking of Bandit when he went to sleep to bring him into the dream. So he figured that by cuddling his soft toy Phinny and thinking of Phinn as he went to sleep, that they would connect up. He was right.

There's warm blue sea to the horizon in every direction, sunshine and fluffy white clouds high overhead, and a soft breeze flipping up white foam on the crests of the waves. A peaceful scene. But Kai can see that Phinn is far from peaceful. He's swimming back and forth in an unusual oval pattern with his dorsal fin flopping over dejectedly. His beak has lost its usual cheeky expression. His eyes are downcast.

"Phinn!" Kai calls. "What's going on? Are you okay?"

Suddenly there's a mighty flash and the sky is alive with glistening light as a shimmering white creature catapults out of the ocean, spinning and turning, somersaulting and diving, then crashing back into the watery world in an explosion of energy.

"Wow!" is all Kai can exclaim, rocked at this extraordinary display of power.

"Meet the Snow Dolphin," says Phinn with the wave of a flipper.

"Oh! Cool!" says Kai, intrigued to meet his dream

guide's boss.

"No, it's not supercool... I'm in trouble." Phinn swims over and sits up spy-hopping to speak with Kai. "She tells me I've gone beyond the boundaries of a dream guide and my assignment will be terminated."

"What! You mean we won't be able to meet any more?" says Kai, suddenly feeling deeply sad.

Phinn nods his beak up and down, too upset to speak.

"But why?"

Phinn takes a few moments to gather his emotions... "My assignment is to be your dream guide. To help you bring through dolphin wisdom to serve the planet."

Kai looks at Phinn and feels the deep bond between them as the dolphin continues, "But I tried to change things for you in a way that wasn't for the good of another human."

"Phinn, you don't mean the boy from Finland, do you? Were we in Finland last night?"

Phinn nods his beak.

"And it was the dogpoo that did it, right?"

Phinn nods again.

"But how did you make it...like, out of the dream and into the physical?"

"Turnin' turtles! It's sometimes possible to do natural magic by concentrating hard and visualising an outcome."

Kai is wide-eyed with wonder.

"It turns things golden – the best that they can be."

"Wow!"

Phinn continues, "I blame my ego, Degbert...of course... He got carried away with wanting to control things."

"Oh, Phinn... You did it for me..."

Just then, the water draws back in front of them and a glistening white beak appears, followed by a sleek dolphin body which oozes shimmering light. Kai finds himself looking into the most amazing eyes he's ever seen. It's like he's seeing beyond time into everything that ever existed in the past or will exist in the future.

"I am the Snow Dolphin. I speak for all dolphins. We greet you in the matrix of love, Young Human!" The sound of her words is almost like music – clear and spacious.

Kai is unsure how to greet such an angelic being, so smiles uncertainly, hoping she'll say more about herself.

She does.

"I am a wise spirit dolphin of ancient times. I have, for many moons, lived high on the snow slopes of Hawaii's White Mountain. The crystal structure of the frozen water in this sacred place has long held dolphin resonance in balance, enabling us to oversee the vast oceans below. And from here, as guardians of the world, to hold peace."

Kai listens enthralled.

"But now, the physical home of my spirit is under threat from rising temperatures, due to disrespect of the natural systems. The pure vibration melts with the snow. And so also the voice of the dolphins, and our connection to life on Earth. It is a time of great change, of species helping each other move forward."

Kai somehow understands the importance of this.

"So," she continues, "it is the time when the dolphins must release their knowledge. And so also it is the time to call up the prophecy of the ancients that states: there will come a boy, who will catapult the planet into a new era of peace." Her eyes hold his gaze in unfathomably deep pools of wisdom. "This is why we have chosen you, Young Human."

Kai shakes his head, mystified.

The Snow Dolphin adds, "Your vulnerability in the sea brooks no barrier to the voice of the dolphins," and smiles warmly, enveloping him in a relaxing hug of shimmering light that seems to come from gleaming white flippers.

Then she turns to Phinn. "Dream Guide, we see the waves of love between your heart-light and that of your human. You have been given another chance at your assignment."

Phew!

Phinn's cheeky grin returns immediately.

"But, Dream Guide, remember to create with love. Visualise what you want, yes. But surround it with love for the good of all. Then it will flow."

"See it! Be it! See it! Be it!" sings Phinn, as suddenly the Snow Dolphin isn't there any more and there's a dull sort of emptiness where her presence has been, and everything merges into a blanket of sleep.

Kai woke sensing the joy of the Snow Dolphin all through him, and the feeling that anything is possible. He tried visualising himself in Hawaii. Then putting a heart round the picture.

But before long he reminded himself that nothing had changed: I know Dad, and there's no way he'll let me do the race. So it's finished for me. I'm not good enough. That's the end of it.

9

Adventure Begins

Two days later a lot of things had changed. The adventure was in fact just beginning.

Kai walked out of the house as he usually did on his way to school. He hugged Bandit, whispering, "See you in my dreams." In his school rucksack were his PE kit, lunch, phone, homework, and today an extra one of his belongings – his much loved soft toy. Hopefully none of the kids at school would notice.

He hadn't taken into account Mum's determination and resourcefulness, from the restrictions of her ailing body and wheelchair. And the ability of her mobile phone to organise. A small tear squeezed its way down his cheek as he thought of the trouble she'd be in for enabling him to be on the race without letting Dad know. There was no doubt he'd be furious when he found out after work that day. Hopefully not violent. He might even call the police. Too late by then. Assuming everything goes to plan.

An excited Luke and ecstatic Daniella bounced up to him as he walked. "Calm down guys!" he said nervously. "No one must know for as long as possible. But thanks, Luke, for having Bandit for me."

"It'll be cool… Me an' Bandit'll have fun practising football moves."

"And, Dani, please thank your mum for looking after my mum."

"Sure… My mum's between jobs and needs something to do anyway. I'll help her."

At that moment Kai realised that having supportive friends was the most important thing on the planet. Even better than double-cheese pizzas.

After tutor group signing-in Mr Jellyman said

to Kai, "See you in the car park at breaktime." He looked anxious. With good reason... If things went wrong his job was on the line. But he felt sure there wasn't much point in dedicating his life to education if he couldn't get the kids to fulfil their potential. And he believed this was the right course of action for Kai to be given a chance to prove himself.

Breaktime came and Kai was whizzed off by Mr Jellyman in his car, changing into his t-shirt, trackies and trainers as they went. Now he didn't look like a schoolboy running away any more, but just a kid off to take part in a race. At the station he boarded the train.

"So," Mr Jellyman instructed, "the contestant from Ireland is called Lana and her mum will meet you in London and make sure you connect up with others for the train to the air base where Mr Dung will meet you. He's the philanthropist behind the race and he will explain everything."

"What's a philanthropist?"

"It's someone who puts up a lot of money to help the world."

"Okay."

"So, here, I've written down all the phone numbers. Oh, and I almost forgot, here is your passport that your mother gave me when we signed the paperwork."

Mr Jellyman held out his hand. "Good luck,

young Kai Duckworth. Be the best that you can be!"

Kai shook hands shyly. It felt strange shaking hands with a teacher. But then there were a lot of strange things happening lately.

Looking out of the window at the green fields of England passing by gave him a feeling of being mesmerised into another reality. Almost a dream, happening too fast to believe. Was he really on the way to Hawaii? In the middle of the Pacific Ocean! On the other side of the world! It was unbelievably exciting and he kept looking around uneasily at all the strangers in the carriage, unable to relax.

A feeling of vulnerability suddenly came in. Of being all by himself. On the run. He really was all alone. It was scary.

He delved into his rucksack to eat the sandwiches in his lunchbox and spotted Phinny, his hand touching the softness. It brought to his mind the dolphin words, 'We're here now. Be ready for adventure'. Instantly he felt better and not quite so alone.

At the London ticket barrier a tall pale girl with plaited red hair, soft green eyes and faded dungarees floated up to him. "Hey Egghead. I'm Lana. Fancy running up a mountain?"

He was taken aback by her nickname aimed at the shape of his head, but somehow her warm smile made up for it and he knew he liked her.

"Feed me and I'll run to the moon and back. I'm starving," he replied, as though he'd known her all his life. It was a good meeting.

Her mum whisked them across London and onto the platform for the next train, with piles of honey sandwiches and cucumbers. Things were looking up.

Here they were joined by a tough-looking bald guy in a grey suit and tie who introduced himself as Security, while busy on his phone. And with him was another of the contestants. She was from Russia. Unnervingly, her eyes stared them down with the look of a polar bear out hunting.

"Hi, I'm Victorica, but you can call me Victa." She wore a black jumpsuit, showing off muscular arms, and stood stiffly holding out a hand to Kai, shaking his so forcefully that Kai had to hide his face from Lana, knowing he had a giggle just waiting to escape.

In the meantime Security had also gathered the two contestants arriving from Africa. "Right, so this is Moz from Somaliland..." he said, roughly pushing forward a boy with a nasty scar down one side of his face, wearing a cap back to front. He looked mean, glaring menacingly at everyone.

"And..." Security waved at a dark-skinned girl, "here's Bibi from South Africa." She had wide afro hair and an arrogant expression. And didn't even bother to look at them as she struggled to climb onto the train, reminding Kai of the way Bandit moved.

"So we have you five kids and the others will join us later."

By the time they'd sat staring at each other for a few minutes on the train they'd all acknowledged their fellow adventurers, and were eying each other up competitively.

"How come you were chosen?" Kai asked Lana.

She shrugged, flipping her plaits over her shoulders, and replied in her lilting Irish brogue, "A bit strange really… I'm a good runner, yes, but I think it's because I'm in tune with plants… I understand what's going on with them."

"How d'you do that?"

"I talk to the nature fairies of course, Egghead."

"Oh, of course…"

"How about you? Why were you chosen?"

"I was just a last minute fill-in."

"That's not what I heard…"

"What did you hear?"

"I heard you speak with dolphins."

Kai was too surprised to reply.

But Victa, pulling herself upright, said in her heavy monotone accent, "Haa! I was chosen for serious reasons. I'm from High Arctic – best junior runner in whole of Russia. I practise with life-force in body to run fast, and to bond with powerful animals like bear, wolf and tiger. And of course to be martial arts champion."

"Cool..." said Kai, making a mental note not to argue with Victa. Nor the Somali boy, Moz, who remained quiet but clenched his fists scornfully. He got the feeling those fists would do a vicious job in a fight. Nor would he want to cross swords with the South African girl, Bibi, who merely muttered, "I see dragons," as though not expecting anyone to believe her. She then continued to glare daggers at everyone.

What is this race? thought Kai. Have I bitten off more than I can chew? I can get on with Lana, but how come everyone else looks like they want to flatten me?

10
The Philanthropist

Kai became more anxious when his mobile started ringing repeatedly as the train drew up at a station. I'm certainly not answering that, he thought, as he got down from the train. That'll be Dad. He bit his lip nervously.

The philanthropist, Mr Dung, met them with a huge smile from under his cowboy hat, and wide-open arms. His eyes looked somewhat Chinese but as soon as he spoke, his American drawl left no doubt about his origins. "Gee, you guys... It's so great to see you. This race is going to be great. You'll love it. We're going to do great things for the planet." Though he was small in stature everything else about him was big.

"Gee, that's great!" said Bibi in a mocking, egotistical way, the exact opposite to the open-hearted Mr Dung.

Mr Dung just smiled, saying quietly, "You've all been chosen for special reasons that'll help others on the planet, so I'm hoping you'll eventually see beyond your own egos." And carried on loudly, "Now, I'm sure you've got questions, but we're behind schedule and the flight crew are waiting, so we're going to drive to the airfield and board the most amazing plane you've ever seen. When we've been in the air for an hour, I'll explain things."

That really is great, thought Kai. Let's get going before Dad can find us and stop me.

They were ushered into a minivan and taken to a low-key military airbase in the middle of a pine forest. Here there was an old runway – the sort deer might wander onto. They drew up alongside a spanking new shiny aircraft, not a bit like the international jet that Kai was expecting. It was small and thin, and along its sides were bright yellow logos inscribed First Net Zero.

"All aboard!" shouted Mr Dung as steps were wheeled up by a tractor.

"And bag inspection!" Security ordered, checking in each of their rucksacks. Hope he doesn't find Phinny, worried Kai, but the soft toy was the first thing that Security pulled out and held up for everyone to see. "Who have we here? A stowaway!" There was sniggering. Kai was mortified. It was all he could do to stop himself running off into the forest.

The attention turned to Moz, who didn't have a rucksack but was frisked by Security, who found a lethal-looking knife tucked into his belt. "That's mine! Give it back!" shouted Moz as Security removed it.

"You'll have it back after the flight, young man," said Security firmly.

Moz, it seemed, was close to tears. That knife was obviously important to him, as though it was all he possessed.

"And I'll take care of your passports and mobiles," ordered Security. "No mobiles ensures the competition is fair for everyone. Your families will be kept up to date. There were mutterings of disapproval from the other kids. But Kai, glancing at the eight incoming calls from Dad, was more than happy to hand his over. Though pangs of guilt hit him. Was he doing the right thing by Mum? Would she be okay?

"C'mon Egghead," said Lana, picking up on his unease. "We're gonna enjoy this." And pushing him up the steps and into a window seat, she sat down next to him. Victa, Moz and Bibi all chose to sit by themselves.

Like a big bird, the plane pottered a little, gathered speed along the bumpy runway before soaring steadily upwards into the evening sky, nice-as-you-like above the English countryside. Then headed west to North America.

Kai relaxed for the first time since leaving home and, even though he didn't mean to, he dozed off, his head lolling against the window.

There's water sloshing somewhere… And a giggling clicking sound…

"Kai, we're here now. Be ready for adventure!"

"Okay Phinn. Don't rub it in. You were right. I'm on an adventure. But some of the other kids are kinda tough. I'm a bit scared of them, to be honest."

"They've never had any love in their lives."

"I guess…"

"But if I was you, I wouldn't trust…"

Bang! A loud explosion.

A bomb?

Kai woke with a start, wiping sharp pieces of something with a chemical smell from his face. "What's going on?"

Lana was laughing uncontrollably. He saw her covered in crisps and licking bits off her hands, which held a split plastic wrapper. "Hey, Egghead, did you know you can explode crisp packets in planes?"

He shook his head and laughed too. That was when Security came up, looking annoyed, to see what the noise was about, just as Lana banged another packet bulging with atmospheric pressure. Too late: Security ended up with bits of crisps all over his nice smart suit.

11
Interconnecting Rings

The plane was holding time with a lingering sun as Mr Dung, still wearing his cowboy hat and a big smile, stood in the aisle before them.

"Well guys, isn't this great?! Apologies for all the secrecy, but it was vital we got this plane in the air before news spread."

Everyone sat up and listened.

"I'm excited to report that this is a big moment for the world. It will change the course of climate change history. We're on the very first net zero flight across the Atlantic, using an entirely carbon-free jet fuel!"

"Waste fuel!" shouted Victa.

"I'm not at liberty to say what fuel, but good thinking."

Victa's face had a smile on it, admittedly a smug one, but it was another first!

"We have to be cautious due to factions who don't want this ground-breaking new technology to happen." Mr Dung turned to the bald scowling man busy on a crisp-removal job. "So, I would ask that you do what Security here says, as he is keeping us all safe."

There was a sense of grumbling resentment among the kids.

"So your job…" he looked optimistically around the small cabin of the plane, "when this baby gets us to Hawaii…is to give us the greatest race ever witnessed… Thirteen-year-old kids…running… up the world's tallest mountain. To promote First Net Zero, this great step forward to help the Natural World Crisis, and focus the world's eyes on a hopeful future for our planet. There's a very substantial prize for the winner! I know you can all do it!"

The feeling changed to one of excitement and

confidence.

"Why thirteen-year-olds?" asked Bibi.

"Yes, why us?" added Lana.

A shadow seemed to come across Mr Dung's face and he paused for a moment, acknowledging the question with the wave of a hand before continuing, "We're working with the Olympic slogan – faster, higher, stronger, together. And we have a girl and a boy representing each of the five Olympic continents depicted by the five rings… Like these, see…"

He handed the kids each a white hoodie and t-shirt emblazoned with the Olympic interconnecting rings in green, blue, red, yellow and black. Underneath was the slogan and the First Net Zero logo.

"The US boy and Colombian girl will be joining us soon from the Americas. And the two from Oceania – that's Australia and the Pacific – and the other Asian will meet us in Hawaii. So, get to know each other."

Kai proudly tried his hoodie on. He couldn't wait to show his friends at home. The kit seemed to announce that this adventure was actually happening. It wasn't a dream.

But something was about to happen that would make him wish it was…

12
Fly-by-night

Somewhere in the night they landed in North America – upstate New York – in a quiet corner of a military airbase with US airforce staff rushing about. Everyone was allowed to stretch their legs and eat hamburgers and fries in a canteen. Then, they waited for the US boy, who'd been delayed. Kai, dead-tired, was now feeling anxious about being on this whole adventure thing, so he curled up on a padded bench, rucksack as a pillow, and closed his eyes.

There's a familiar voice. "We're here now. Be ready for adventure."

It looks like they're in a swimming pool. The underwater lights are casting a strange glow on a dark shape moving along propelled by tail flukes surging up and down. It's too confined a space for such a motion, designed for wide open seas.

"Phinn! What are you doing here?"

"Hi Kai. Thought I'd try out the airforce training pool. Turnin' turtles! It's far too small. No idea how they work in this."

"They're humans you know."

"Yes, such a puny species, especially for one that thinks it's so important."

"Phinn, did you come here to be rude?"

"Sorry. Dumpin' dogfish! That's my ego, Degbert, taking over again. No, listen, I want to show you something. Follow me...and be really quiet."

"Phinn, we're in a dream. How can anyone awake actually hear us?"

"You may be right, but I don't want to take any chances. C'mon!"

Kai floats in his dream body after the dolphin, outside to the airfield, where they hover by a fence near the shadowy outline of the plane.

"Look... See?"

"I can't see. It's dark, dopey."

"Who're you calling dopey?"

"Phinn, humans can't see in the dark," says Kai grumpily.

"You're getting stroppy now... Turnin' turtles! If you can't see that person bending over the wheel with a spanner then that's too bad. I'm off!"

"Phinn! Phinn! Where are you? Phinn!"

He's not here.

"Kai! Wake up!" Lana was shaking his shoulder. "You were shouting!"

"Where's Phinn?"

"Who?"

"Oh, sorry... He's my dream guide."

"Cool... Listen. Sit up. The American boy, Hank, is here. He arrived in a huge long posh car. We've got to get back on the plane."

"Swanky hanky eh?"

Lana giggled. "C'mon!"

They joined the other kids waiting outside near the plane, now lit brightly with searchlights. The new contestant was there. He was a boy immaculately dressed in a smart shirt with chinos and trendy trainers. His hair was cut short except for the bit at the front which stuck up, and even though it was the middle of the night he wore sunglasses. "Hey guys!" he called, confidently walking over to shake hands. "The name's Hank. Junior US gold medalist for 1,500 metres."

Kai didn't think 'Kai, washing-up champion' was such a good reply so just nodded as they were ushered up the steps to the plane. He was about to sit down when he remembered… "I've just gotta check something…" He pushed past everyone and rushed down the steps and round to underneath the plane where he could see the wheels. He studied them for a while with no idea what he was looking for, but he knew he had to look. They looked like…well…like wheels.

"Hey, you! Kai… What're you doing?" It was the unmistakably irritating voice of Security. "Get back on the plane immediately."

Kai shrugged and went back up to his seat. But they didn't take off. Instead there seemed to be some sort of commotion, with Mr Dung and Security deep in discussion.

After a while Mr Dung came and spoke to the kids. "I'm sorry to say there's been a worrying disruption going on. The wheels have been tampered with. Luckily we've now checked them, all is back in order and we're cleared to go. But it could've been a nasty accident. One of you kids was spotted near the wheels. You know who you are. Please come and speak to me later."

Mr Dung continued to look at everyone. But Security stared pointedly at Kai. And so everyone else then stared pointedly at Kai. "I haven't done anything," he mumbled, shrinking into his seat.

"It's disappointing," said Mr Dung. "But we need to get on the way now."

Kai felt as though a lead weight had just landed on his chest. Why was he being accused? "Lana, you believe me don't you?" he asked.

She looked at him sadly. "I'm not sure what to think, Egghead… You did go back down the steps…"

This was bad. It was like he'd just been swallowed by a deep dark black hole with a lid clamped down on top. He'd never felt so lost, ever. He retreated into himself. He missed Bandit badly. And desperately wanted to cuddle his soft toy, Phinny, but didn't dare. He just hugged the rucksack and slumped into his seat.

Then, a small bright thought: he could talk to Phinn.

As the plane droned on through the night, he closed his eyes and dozed. There didn't seem to be any dreams. There was no sign of Phinn. He'd been rude to him. He'd gone.

He felt completely alone.

13
Dream Stones

Time appeared to stand still as they travelled on west. It was still dark when they landed on a California military base on the US Pacific coast. They stretched their legs and nibbled on cornbread and deep-fried cake, and drank orange juice. Everyone was overtired, and couldn't wait to finally get to Hawaii. Nobody spoke to Kai. Indeed it seemed that the others were going out of their way to avoid him. It was even worse when both Victa and Moz glared meanly at him. This really upset him. He was sure they were aware that Security was watching him like a hawk.

After endless checks they were back in their seats and ready for the final leg. It only increased his misery when Lana decided to sit next to Bibi.

However, the new contestant from South America plonked herself down next to Kai, "Hola... I'm Josee-Marie from Colombia." He couldn't help noticing how beautiful she was, with tanned skin, brown eyes and dark hair swept up in a colourful band. She was warm, and friendly to match. And soon, as the plane droned on across the Pacific Ocean through the long night, she had Kai telling her all about the journey and the accusation of sabotaging the wheels.

"Oh, I shouldn't worry too much about that," she said. "Where I come from there's so much crime that you're strange if no one suspects you of anything! My village grows coca plants for the drug barons... There's too much poverty to do anything else."

Kai looked at her, awestruck.

"I never knew my parents, I grew up on the streets, so I've had to learn to be strong and true to myself and those who help me. And I discovered

I have a useful sense of smell for things that aren't right. It got me an education – and onto this race. I'm determined to win the prize money so I can help my village."

Her fiery confidence rubbed off on him. She'd obviously had to fight to get here. It made him feel what an easy life he'd had.

He stopped feeling so sorry for himself and leaned back. His eyes, heavy with sleep, drifted to the cabin window. A full moon was shining down onto luminous clouds that looked like an endless sea.

A dark-grey triangle cuts through the gleaming water, heading his way.

"Hi Kai. We're here now..."

"Phinn! I missed you. I wasn't sure you'd come back."

"Turnin' turtles! I missed you too."

Dolphin flippers grab the boy in a hug and they roll over and over, laughing as they come up for air.

"I'm sorry I was grumpy, Phinn."

"I'm sorry too." His big tail kerplooshes wildly, engulfing them both in a waterfall. "You know, Kai, the Snow Dolphin told me that when things don't make sense, you have to listen to your heart."

"Okay… How do I do that?"

"Dumpin' dogfish! You pay attention to the song singing inside you."

"Oh…but how do I find that? I've been feeling so bad, there's nothing singing inside. I almost forgot I was on an exciting adventure – and even wanted to go home…"

"So what makes you feel good now?"

"I don't know. There's so much rushing about my head…"

"Ignore that. Put your flippers – hands will have to do – on your heart and think of something lovely, like a hug with your dog… And listen."

"Hmm." Kai pondered… "Going home with the prize money which'll help my mum."

"Supercool! So that's your heart-song."

"Okay."

"C'mon… I want to show you how to dive for pebbles. Take a deep breath, hold on to my flipper and see yourself at the bottom of the ocean. We'll start off shallow…"

Kai finds himself on a sunny seabed, among fronds of wavy brown seaweed and different types of fish swimming by. They pass over rocky homes of bright beautiful creatures, large and small, bubbles from them catching the light, rising to the surface above.

Phinn uses his beak to snuffle up a carpet of shells and sand, creating a cloud. "Here, see those reddish pebbles... Can you reach them?"

Kai waits for a gap in the cloud, and grabs a handful, nestling beside a clump of green seagrass. Then realises he's being propelled to the surface to gulp air.

"You okay?" Josee was staring at him. "You're breathing funny."

"Yeah… I was…just dreaming…thanks." Kai felt disorientated being back in the plane. He was about to shut his eyes again, when suddenly he opened them wide with astonishment.

His hand was clutching three little pebbles.

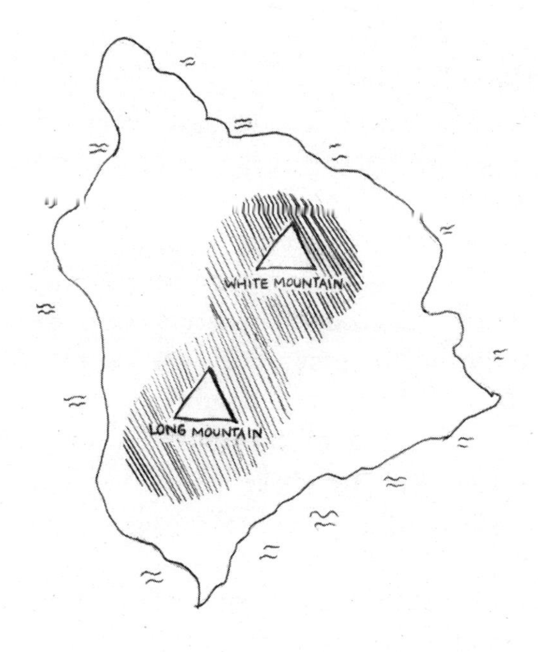

14
Hello Hawaii

Out of the cabin window Kai could see the glow of a dawning pink sun as the plane lost height and banked away from the inky sky, alongside a huge purple storm cloud which billowed white and orange at its base.

They were coming down to the islands of Hawaii, a land of colour. And, he felt, surely a land of secret and magic.

"Hey kids!" called Mr Dung, "This is the Big Island. Here, we're the furthest away from any land mass on Earth – just Pacific Ocean for a couple of thousand miles in all directions."

The sky was lightening enough to see the outline of the island and get a sense that it was largely two great mountains rising out of the sea.

"To the north, that's our race target, White Mountain – the tallest on Earth."

Kai got a sense of the enormity of it. And the enormity of the challenge he had agreed to undertake to run up it. How ridiculous! But how exciting!

"To the south is Long Mountain, where we'll be training – the largest mountain mass there is. Both are volcanos measured from their base on the ocean floor."

Kai stared in wonder.

"Look," said Mr Dung. "Can you see spewing ash clouds and tracks of lava? Like rivers… From the longest erupting volcano on the planet."

This was also an unstable land.

Kai was pondering how it would be to live near erupting land… And how would his adventure go… And would he be able to get on with the other kids…when… Thump! The wheels touched down on tarmac and brought the plane firmly to a halt.

Josee tapped Kai on the shoulder and pointed to Mr Dung, who was wiping tears from his face. He spotted them looking at him and smiled. "It's been a lot of hard work getting this inaugural flight off the ground – in more ways than one," he said to them.

"Mr Dung," said Kai. "About before… I was only looking at the wheels. I didn't touch them."

Mr Dung nodded. "Okay… There's been a few funny things happening – like with Hank's family car, which was why he was late. C'mon, let's get off and through passport control." Kai felt reassured that he might be believed. It was Security and the other kids he still had to convince.

Walking across the tarmac was like walking through honey. The air was sweet and as thick as swimming through water in a dream. And with a brain craving sleep it could well have been a dream. As they walked towards open-air buildings in the shape of thatched huts, past gently swaying palm trees, Kai felt a friendly presence beside him. It was Lana. "I know you didn't do it, Egghead," she whispered.

"How d'you know?"

"The nature fairies here are telling me."

"How do they know?"

"They see your heart-light," she said.

"That's what my dream guide says," he smiled. "Here, look…" He pulled the red pebbles out of his pocket and showed her. "What do your nature fairies think about my dream-stones?"

She moved towards a large plant pot of scented yellow hibiscus flowers and shut her eyes for a minute. A stripy butterfly as big as a hand fluttered nearby with an army of dragonflies. "They say you should carry them on your run to the top of the mountain. That way, you're connecting the base below the ocean to the summit and honouring the nature fairies across the whole mountain."

Kai nodded, trying to take the information in.

She continued, "It's important. They say we have to be in tune with the land here, like the native Hawaiians."

He wasn't quite sure what this meant, but had no time to think about it as Victa jogged by with her nose in the air.

Followed by Moz swaggering, hands in pockets, sneering, "Oh no! That teddy bear's going to be kidnapped…"

Kai remembered the knife and tried to ignore him.

Then Bibi wandered past with her peculiar gait, one hip at a different angle to the other, definitely off-balance somehow. "Hey, Lana… Don't talk to him. He's a loser." She glared at Kai.

"I'll catch you in a minute," Lana replied, turning to Kai. "Did you know she's only got one leg?"

Surprised, Kai shook his head.

"She says she lost a leg after being attacked by a gang in South Africa…'cos of being different… like seeing dragons and stuff. Explains why she doesn't like people. She says her only friends are dragons."

Hearing the stories of some of the other kids made him feel heavy inside. Turning, he looked back. There was the arc of a huge rainbow around the plane. At least the land was welcoming him.

By the time they had been through customs he felt more relaxed, as he realised the new contestants joining them knew nothing about his journey. And anyway, some of the others might feel as nervous as he did.

Mr Dung introduced them to the Oceania representatives. "Now y'all, this here is Wilga from Australia." He touched the arm of a bare-footed girl with chocolate brown skin, a broad nose and a mop of wild blond hair. Her dark eyes darted to and fro like a wild animal. "G'day," she shyly said.

"And here we have Tane from the Pacific Islands of Kiribati." He waved at a boy who looked as though he'd just come out of the ocean, much like the Hawaiians – handsome, large-boned and strong. He was smiling confidently, entirely at ease in bright-coloured shorts and flip-flops, with a shark's tooth thong around his neck.

Kai was pleased when Mr Dung produced shorts for all of them. It was already hot and sticky, even this early in the morning. But he wasn't prepared for the warm greeting outside the airport.

"Welcome to the land of peace and love – the land of aloha," said men in flowery shirts and women in grass skirts with flowers in their hair, giving the arrivals large necklaces of fresh flowers known as leis. The kids had no choice. They were soon all adorned, apart from Moz, who tore his off with a "Euw!"

Then they were attacked by people with cameras, and journalists mobbing them with questions about the flight and the race.

"Of course, this First Net Zero flight was the most expensive ever," boasted the US boy, Hank, enjoying the attention.

"I shall win the race for Russia," bragged Victa.

Security hustled them through to a waiting eco-minibus while Mr Dung held court with the media, manfully trying to answer all the questions, over-twirling his cowboy hat and getting his lei completely tangled.

Newspapers across the world the next day would show the kids in their First Net Zero t-shirts and Mr Dung gasping for breath, being throttled by a garland of flowers.

15
Shark

In a dream-like daze, Kai looked out of the window of the minibus as they drove towards the town near the airport. This was the western side of the island – the dry side – so the sky was typically clear and blue and Kai could see across the open desert scrub to mountains on one side and sea on the other.

He was more interested in food, but luckily Mr Dung had managed to gather some breakfast of local fish sticks, sweet bread and tomato ketchup. This kept them going while getting a feel for the land they were in.

"Gee… Great! There's a lava tube. That's a tunnel made by a river of hot melted rock coming out of the earth," said Mr Dung, pointing at a dark cave by the side of the road. "Remember, this island may be known as paradise with its turquoise sea and beautiful beaches, but it's actively volcanic. Things change all the time. It's good to respect the natural systems."

They pulled up at a wide bay with a white sandy beach, tourist shops and restaurants brightly displayed along a promenade. Locals were preparing themselves for a busy day with holiday folk.

"I'm going to pick up our last contestant," said Mr Dung. "So I'll leave you here with Security. I'm sure you can amuse yourselves for a while."

Security grunted, wiping his sweating bald head with his once-smart suit sleeve and settling himself at a table in a café with his laptop, seemingly uninterested in the kids. They looked at each other, unsure what to do.

"We go for a run," suggested Victa. "Good to train in this heat."

"I'd rather take in a milk shake," said Josee.

"This is the land of opportunity for our stomachs."

"No, c'mon," said Tane, heading off down the beach. "Look, there's a place we can get canoes… Let's go exploring." Everyone eagerly followed, Kai reluctantly at the back, certain he didn't want to go canoeing. Particularly as he was sure he'd be sea-sick. But as Hank paid for them each to have a tiny yellow pointed boat he knew he couldn't possibly be the only one not to. That would be too much to bear.

The renting guy insisted they wear bright orange life-jackets, stating "No wear, no go." Tane reluctantly put his on muttering, "Ridiculous!" But he and Hank, being the only ones to have canoed before, happily showed the others how to use their wooden paddles.

"How hard can this be?" sneered Moz confidently. There were echoes of excitement from the group.

Lana smiled at Kai.

He tried to smile back, conscious already of the fear and the heavy queasy feeling in his tummy. He bit his lip nervously.

The guy pushed them off from the jetty saying, "Stay in the calm waters of the bay. Don't go near the reef." They headed off, splashing, squealing and laughing, canoes tipping back and forth, and he shouted after them, "Away from reef is important. Sighting of tiger shark yesterday! Can be aggressive."

Kai tried to ignore his dry mouth and shaky hands, and concentrate on keeping his weight balanced in the middle. He tried to paddle in a straight line. But his long legs got in the way. And the canoe seemed to have a mind of its own and ended up going along in arcs like a drunken balloon. And every time he tried to correct the direction, he tipped dangerously from side to side. Focus! Focus! he told himself. I can't be left behind. But before long he was aware that the others ahead out in the bay had already turned to follow the inside of the reef marked by white breakers. I must catch up, he chided himself, almost in tears, angry for being so pathetic. By the time he got close to the reef he realised his mistake. Here, where the noise of the ocean increased, the swell was bigger and the canoe tipped even further – almost over. His tummy lurched. The inevitable happened. He vomited repeatedly over the side.

He felt rotten like on the school trip. He couldn't control the rolling of the canoe. And then the next swell swept the paddle overboard. Oh no! What now? Real trouble! He reached as far as he dared to try and grab the wooden end... Nearly...and again...nearly... Then, wham! splash! The canoe seemed to shoot out from underneath him, tipping him headfirst into the water.

The roar of the ocean sounded like screaming, or

was he screaming? Aieee! The life-jacket bobbed him straight up to chaotic explosions in his ears. He was thrashing about, arms flailing in panic...or was it the hurly-burly of the reef?... Was he being carried over it? Would he be smashed?

Instinctively, he started shouting, "Phinn! Phinn! Help!" between mouthfuls of salty slosh.

Then, in utter relief, he spotted a dark-grey fin charging towards him. But in seconds, relief turned to fear. The fin was triangular and sharp. Not curved backwards like a dolphin. It was moving from side to side, not up and down like a dolphin. It was attached to a body twice the length of a man. The body had a gaping mouth with sharp teeth. It came close, hoovering up drifting vomit. Small eye glaring.

Shark!

Hungry shark!

It had the markings of stripes across the back of its body.

Hungry tiger shark!

Kai's chest felt like lead.

Briefly he wondered how Mum and Dad would take the news. He would finally make the headlines! 'Boy taken by vomit-eating shark in Hawaii'. Would Dad even care?

Suddenly he was aware the movement was different. He was being circled. Around and around, he was being circled. A predator playing with its prey. Ready to pounce…

But then there were more fins. More and more. Almost in disbelief he became aware that the fins were rounded and moving up and down. Wow! Could it be? Yes! He was definitely being circled by a pod of slimline dolphins. A tight circle of protection that was keeping at bay the thwarted shark beyond.

"We're here now!" said a voice with a clicking giggle in Kai's ear as one of the dolphins sped by with a familiar cheeky grin.

"Phinn! I love you," he blurted, letting out a long breath he hadn't realised he'd been holding.

One of the dolphins approached the tiger shark and head-butted him fiercely. With a final swipe of his tail and a frustrated glare from his eye, the shark recognised he'd been defeated and swam off, chased by the dolphins. Some of them gave an aerial display, spinning high out of the water as if in triumph.

"Supercool!" wafted over…

At that moment there was a shout. "Hey! You alright?" and a canoe appeared. It was Tane. He skilfully steered up to Kai's upturned canoe and righted it, bringing it alongside Kai. Then he grabbed Kai by his life-jacket and hauled him back on board while Hank arrived and managed to steady the canoes.

Then came the other kids, with Bibi shouting,

"Stupid idiot!" And Victa saying, "Knew we couldn't trust him."

Tane towed him back to the beach. He was still shaking...but alive!

Wilga quietly came and touched him on the shoulder, with a surprising sense of tiny hands grounding him into his body.

Lana helped him with his canoe. "Living on the edge, to be sure, Egghead! It was Tane who knew you were in difficulties. He raced back to help."

"Thanks, mate," Kai said to Tane. "I owe you."

"It was nothing. I'm stronger than you and used to the sea," Tane replied, fingering the shark's tooth talisman of sea power at his neck. "Great Sea Spirit told me to come back for you. He sings to me. People say he sings in my blood. Hah! But I wasn't expecting that tiger. If it hadn't've been for the dolphins..."

"Dolphins are special."

"Yeah. I've heard of that happening before. Interesting how the dolphins help humans when in need...and what do we humans do? We chuck rubbish in their home, ruin their lives with ship noises, and kill them..."

"It's also the home of the shark," said Wilga. "He was just doing what sharks do."

"Yup, going around clearing up vomit..."

They laughed and scooted sand at each other. Then ran up the beach, finding an old football to kick around.

It didn't take long for the sun to dry them off.

Security didn't seem to have noticed what they'd been doing and hadn't moved from his table at the café. Though he did whip his laptop lid down quickly, looking smug as they approached.

The kids, although already fiercely competitive with each other, were united by age and, as if by common agreement, didn't mention what they'd been doing.

When Mr Dung came back with the minibus he asked, "So what have you guys been up to?"

"Nothing much. Just getting to know the locals…"

"Okay. Great! This here is Choekyi, our other representative from Asia – from Tibet in the Himalayas. Our team is now complete."

The boy with Mr Dung put his hands on his heart and said, "Tashi Delek. Hello." He was thin and fragile-looking and fiddled awkwardly with his shorts as though this was the first time he'd ever worn western clothes. Kai didn't think he could even run to the end of the street. But behind long black hair he noticed brown eyes that stared at him with an expression he couldn't quite place. And he had an uncomfortable feeling that Choekyi connected to people at a deep level, so somehow knew everything he was thinking.

They drove north a little way, seeing beautiful beaches, some with volcanic black sand, some with peaceful waters inhabited by snorkellers and some with massive waves that had Tane oohing and aahing to join the surfers. This was, after all, the surfing capital of the world. But they drove on, past macadamia nut orchards and climbing east across green cattle country until, higher still, they emerged onto swathes of dark lava desert.

They were on the middle road that cuts between White Mountain and Long Mountain. "This is military land," said Mr Dung. "The locals won't stop here. They say strange magic happens."

"What sort of things?" asked Josee, sitting up in interest.

"UFOs, for starters…"

"Oh, them. We get those in the Andes," she replied, sitting back.

"Watch out for Hawaii's own special magic," Mr Dung laughed.

As if on cue, mist swirled in suddenly and, in contrast to the recent sunlit coast, they found themselves peering across a barren moonscape.

They stopped at a junction and clambered out to look.

"So, guys…this is where you'll be running up on the race." Mr Dung pointed north. "It may look gentle but don't be fooled. I can assure you it's pretty steep. And even though this is summer, and snow incredibly rare, it's seriously cold up there." Through the drifting mists they could see the sky had been overtaken by the arc of a huge dome littered with baby volcanos known as cinder cones. This was the great White Mountain. The tallest mountain in the world. Kai felt a mesmerising powerful energy about it. He stared, trying to imagine what he'd taken on.

"We're at 2,000 metres above sea level here... So almost half way to the summit... But, up there," Mr Dung pointed skywards, "there's less air pressure, so considerably less oxygen. That's what will challenge you."

"Easy!" said Victa. "I will make Russia proud."

"Can't wait to get at it," said Hank. "This is home soil. I will win for the US!"

They glared at each other. The competitive spirit was firing warning shots.

"Hawaii wasn't always American was it?" asked Josee.

"No," replied Hank. "Not before around the beginning of the last century. That's when my great grandfather was born here. The US took over and my family lost their land to pineapple plantations and became so poor they were like slaves and had to stowaway on a boat to the mainland. When I heard that as a child, I swore I'd never be poor."

"Do you feel a bit Hawaiian?" asked Tane.

"No, not really," Hank said, then paused.

"'Cept...well, there is one funny thing that happens..." He looked embarrassed.

"What?" asked Wilga.

"Well... You know for Hawaiians the spirit of the ancestors is important... So...there are times when my great grandfather seems to speak through me... Mostly when I'm under pressure. I start speaking in a sort of gruff voice and saying old-fashioned stuff."

"Woohoo!" said Moz. And everyone laughed.

"But being a bit Hawaiian, I'm a dead cert to beat you all and win the race," said Hank with a big grin.

Kai listened to Hank's story with no confidence of his own. He'd nothing to gauge the experience against. This was the first mountain he'd ever been on. The pit of his stomach was jumping up and down with nerves. That would be his first challenge to cope with. Beyond that, he'd have to just wait and see.

The middle road took them on and down eventually into green land again – the wonderful, lush tropical vegetation of the east coast – and to the sprawling old main town. It was raining but that didn't spoil the loveliness of the wooden buildings and brightly coloured flowers everywhere. They'd stepped out of a desert into a rainforest.

The travellers' hostel where they were staying welcomed them warmly, as did the resident scruffy grey cat. They relaxed with drinks in old but comfy rattan chairs with well-worn cushions, on a verandah open to the call of frogs and night birds. The cat walked around inspecting each of them and finally decided to sit on Choekyi's lap. Someone produced a guitar and there was easy singing, bringing them all together as a group.

But Kai was too tired to care about anything except a rapid meal and sleep. Jet-lag had finally caught up with him. He'd come half way across the world from home and was exhausted.

At last he fell into his bed in the room he was sharing with the boys. Grabbing Phinny as secretly as he could from his rucksack, he curled up with him under the covers and shut his eyes. But he'd been spotted. Moz scoffed, "Oh no, we've got to share a room with the baby! We must do something about that teddy bear."

Kai had been warned. But sleep was all that mattered.

16
Help!

Bash! Clump! Plonk! There's no room to move. Kai pushes and kicks. Out of my way! Give me space! But more stuff bumps up against him. Sloshing up and down. He's aware that the stuff is firm but shifts around easily.

Then he can see. He appears to be in the ocean. Certainly he's close to a shore with mountains beyond. And he's bobbing up and down. But it's in a rubbish tip. All around him are bits of plastic – bottles, cups and bright-coloured broken toys, with brandnames on, saying 'Buy me'…

"Kai! We're here now," a distressed voice says. "Not much of an adventure, this..."

"Phinn!! How are you?"

"Dumpin' dogfish! Not good here. Have a quick look and let's go."

"Where are we?"

"The southern coast of the Big Island. Where all the currents come together and bring in huge amounts of waste plastic. Look. It's even piled up all over the beach there."

"It's horrible."

"Turnin' turtles! The worst thing is that neither the dolphins nor any of the sea creatures can live in it...broken down to tiny bits and part of the sea...like plastic soup. This kills them."

"But that's dreadful!"

"Yup." Phinn angrily shoves away a broken plastic games console with his flipper. "The dolphins want me to show you."

"So, where does it come from?"

"From across the entire planet. Humans everywhere are trying to throw away plastic that doesn't decompose. Sometimes it gathers in patches the size of countries! It pollutes land, sea and air."

A dark turtle shape appears, trying to force its way through the mess, shaking strangely. There's a plastic bag stuck over its head. Kai shoves his way round and manages to remove the bag. At this point he remembers what Dad makes at home. Oh no! Plastic bags!

Phinn continues, "Sometimes the sea creatures think those are jellyfish and eat them. That kills them."

The turtle submerges under the worst of the mess and paddles off with a grateful nod.

"They want you to help, Kai. You and the kids."

"But aren't people doing something about it?"

"Yup! Humans on Hawaii work hard every day trying to collect it, but it keeps pouring in. It's the bigger problem that needs answers."

"But how can we help?"

"They say the young humans will find a way..."

"Ugh!" Kai crossly shoves some of the stuff out of his way.

Thump! Kai's pillow fell on the floor. Then a smaller Phinny-sized thump! Some of the other boys stirred. Kai was wide awake now. He picked up his pillow and hid Phinny in his rucksack. He noticed his plastic toothbrush on the side and touched it thoughtfully.

Looking around, he saw that all the others still seemed to be fast asleep. He pulled on a t-shirt and shorts and crept out.

He sighed. The air smelt divine – better than freshly cooked pancakes – from beautiful scattered flowers. All around there was the tweeting of birds starting their day, accompanied by the buzzing of insects, and the chirping of lizards and noisy tree frogs.

Pushing between large-leafed tropical plants dripping from a recent rain shower, Kai followed a track to a small beach, feeling the exquisite warm sand between his bare toes. He bent to pick up a handful and studied the grains. Yes, he saw unnatural colours and bits of plastic.

The track took him on to an inlet where the sea was dashing happily up against rocks, now sharp on his feet. He sat down, enjoying the feeling of sharing the spray with the ocean. Dawn was just peeking across the bay, as though come to light up paradise. The waves energised him with a warm welcome. He felt at peace.

The next wave washed in visitors – three mottled turtles breakfasting on bright green tangled seaweed. Flippers and tails worked hard to prevent bashing against rocks. Small heads poked up above the surface, gulping air with large inquisitive eyes.

"Oh, beautiful turtles, please don't eat plastic bags!" Kai begged. He couldn't help thinking of Dad making the deadly items day after day. A small tear escaped and ran down his cheek. He brushed it away with the back of his hand, where the wind carried it over the waves to join a passing rainbow.

Back at the hostel he went to find the others. Peering into the room he saw that the boys had already gone for breakfast, beds all in disarray. But he noticed that his rucksack had been moved. I'll just check, he thought in alarm…and looked inside. Then searched under the covers and under the bed and all around his area. Then around the room. And then he looked again.

There was no question.

Phinny had gone!

17
End of the Rainbow

He found the kids in the breakfast area. They were lounging on benches, eating pineapples and waffles with maple syrup. Security was sitting to the side, very red in the face and still in a suit. It appeared he couldn't let go his official I'm-in-charge role and was about to burst into a disciplinary explosion, like a water-balloon.

Moz was looking particularly pleased with himself, chucking bits of food around.

Kai marched up to him, torn by embarrassment, but emboldened by the fear of losing his beloved Phinny. "What've you done with him?" he said angrily.

"Woh!" said Moz unkindly. "Looks like our baby has lost his teddy bear. Oh no! What a shame!"

"Give him back to me!" shouted Kai, grabbing him tightly by the arm.

This was what Moz had been waiting for. He shoved as hard as he could and sent Kai flying across the room. Benches and tables crashed as he went, smashing plates, food and drinks onto the floor. He rolled to a halt against a now-broken plant pot, its beautiful tropical specimen floating in mud strewn in all directions. In seconds Moz was on top of him, fists pounding him in the face.

The others were yelling at Kai, "Get up and fight!" but Security jumped in, forcibly dragging the boys apart shouting, "Delinquents!"

That was when Mr Dung appeared. At least, everyone assumed it was Mr Dung. Nobody recognised the pale forehead and greying hair without its cowboy hat. But his entrance had the effect of calming down the situation and everyone slunk back to their seats.

"I don't wish to know what this is all about," Mr Dung said, looking round at the mess with a wry smile, "but let's all put the room back together – remembering that out of chaos comes harmony. The purpose of our race is to help bring the chaos of the planet into harmony..."

Everyone slunk around tidying up as best they could.

"Great!" Mr Dung continued. "Now...if anyone wants to win this great race, it's to be done with legs and heart. Not fists. We've got training to do. So let's put our energy into that and compete with each other by running."

Moz glared at Kai menacingly.

Kai, black-eyed and bruised, sat down sullenly. He felt a supportive presence beside him. He didn't have to look to know it was Lana.

"So, listen up. I'm going to tell you about our training program. Firstly I want to say, if you don't want to run, don't run... Simple. No-one's forcing you. In normal times, thirteen-year-olds wouldn't be encouraged to run long distances... Certainly not up a mountain at altitude. But these are not normal times. We have a world in environmental crisis. We have to do something out of the ordinary to make people sit up and notice. To say: Look! Young people care about the future of our planet. Adults are wrecking it with policies that create climate change, pollution and loss of our animals. But we want a future... Is that worth fighting for?"

Everyone nodded enthusiastically.

"I said is that worth fighting for?"

"Yeah! Yeah! Yeah!"

"Gee, that's great! Then let's do this! I'm really proud of y'all. Some of you haven't had opportunities before, but I know each of you has the mental capability to do this. To keep going when things get tough… And they will get tough, mark my words. But I believe in each one of you."

Mr Dung looked around, trying to make eye contact with all the kids.

"You each have a different reason for wanting to win the very considerable cash prize. Don't forget it. The training will be boring – you'll want to be off doing things with your friends… So your own important goal will motivate you – help keep you focused. You each have been given this extraordinary opportunity. Make the most of it, so your communities back home can be proud of you, so your countries can be proud of you, so the world can benefit!"

The feeling in the room had changed dramatically. Smiles of purpose were back.

"Right… So… The training plan. We're going to run every day for a few days. Then a longer one – and a rest day. Then repeat the process. You'll be adapting to the temperatures, but most importantly, getting your bodies used to the altitude. That's going to be the most limiting thing on the race. And we don't know who'll cope best, however good a runner you are."

The kids glanced at each other, eyebrows raised. So it wasn't to be the best runner who would win...

"So, we'll spend some time at the Visitors Centre on White Mountain at 2,800 metres. Then have a couple of days climbing Long Mountain, sleeping high at 3,000 and 4,000 metres. Then, after some rest days, will be the race itself... This'll give our bodies the best chance of adapting to the lack of oxygen on the race to the summit of White Mountain at 4,207."

Mr Dung smiled knowingly at Choekyi.

Then he continued, "Most of you are used to training, so you know it's also important to stretch muscles, drink loads of water and eat well. There'll be great food always here at the hostel. And equally important is sleep. Get all you can and respect others' needs."

Kai stole a glance at Moz, who was fiddling with a fork restlessly.

"So... That's about it, I think.... Oh... And we've got the media coming from all round the world so we want to be ready for them."

Mr Dung's rousing words did the trick. Everyone was keen to get into the day's programme. They were soon dressed in trainers, shorts and caps, ready to run. Apart from Lana, who was in long sleeves, trousers and wide hat to protect her pale skin. They assembled outside.

"Today, head south along the beach trail. Keep to about an hour of gentle jogging at your own pace…nice and steady."

No one was listening. Everyone was staring at Bibi, in her bright yellow shorts and vest, matching jacket tied around her waist. Where her left leg should've been she wore a high-tech prosthetic leg – a blade – the kind that Paralympians wear to run at superhuman speeds.

"That's not fair," said Victa loudly.

"Definitely an unfair advantage," said Hank, and everyone muttered in agreement.

"Well, I've been thinking life's unfair ever since losing my leg," said Bibi forcefully. "It's not only that, but the hours and hours of pain getting used to a false one… And I've learnt you just have to put up with it. So there! Stuff it!" She set off, bounding into the distance.

Victa chased after her with a determined look on her face, like a wolf on a night prowl.

Tane, Hank and Moz gave each other a thumbs-up and set off fast in pursuit.

Kai joined Lana, Josee and Wilga, jogging gently along, looking out for interesting plants and birds, while he told them about his plastic dream.

Way back out of sight somewhere was Choekyi.

That afternoon Security took some of the kids in the minibus to investigate a surfing bay. Kai found himself hanging out on the beach near the hostel with Lana, Wilga and Choekyi. They sat watching the sea, idly running fingers through the warm sand trying not to think of its plastic content – what might have been a bike handle or a toilet seat…

Kai watched Choekyi mesmerised by the waves. "Bit different from home, is it?"

Choekyi smiled. "Yes. First time big sea."

"Wow!"

"Where do you live?"

"I live in mountains…in monastery."

"Like a monk?"

"Yes, I am novice monk."

"How come you speak English?"

"Master of monastery taught me… He say important for all peoples to speak together for greater understanding of wisdoms."

"Okay…"

Kai was thinking about this when a voice said from behind, "Aren't you going in to swim? Look, Honu the turtle is there."

Turning ,they saw an old women standing close by. She wore a faded loose top and flowing skirt and her greying hair was held by a ring of leaves and pinpointed with hibiscus flowers. She sat down beside them.

"Aloha!"

"Hi."

There was silence for a while as they watched the sea together. All was relaxed and peaceful. She was right: every now and then they saw bobbing turtle heads.

"Honu is welcoming you," she said. "He's been around a long time… Lived with the dinosaurs…"

Wriggling her bare brown toes, she turned to the kids as if she wanted to say something really important…

"I'm a kahuna."

"What's a kahuna?"

"A native Hawaiian priest or priestess."

"D'you do magic?" asked Lana.

"Well now, that depends on what you call magic, but…" she stared at Kai, "I do know that you have a dolphin boy among you."

They all turned to look at her with interest. She had a smiley wrinkled face that told of finding happiness through hardship.

"It's good what you do," she said. "Bringing attention to peace for Mother Earth…. I know you kids are special… I can see the rainbows."

"Why are there so many rainbows here?"

"It's just a way the natural systems communicate with us… We like to talk story with Mother

Earth… Connecting up with the land, the sea, the sky…"

No one was surprised when a beautiful rainbow spread its wings right in front of them.

"They express joy."

"Mmm… It gives me the same shape feeling inside as when a dolphin jumps," murmured Kai.

"It's the arc," smiled the old woman.

Lana, Wilga and Choekyi were smiling too.

"So… We native Hawaiians would like to be part of your journey up the mountain…honouring this old sacred path."

"Okay."

"The dolphins are leaving signs… They've been gathering… "

"Oh?"

"It's time…"

"Time for what?"

"To bring back some of the old ways… To respect Mother Earth… To act with aloha – with love."

"Ah…"

"Long ago when this land was the land of Mu, we had thousands of species of plants and animals all living happily together. Some call it biodiversity. That's now been lost. So, we must bring it back for our land to survive."

Wilga's eyes shone… "It's the same with my people in Australia, the Aboriginals. The little mimis, the rock spirits, have been telling me all my life to use the old ways..."

"The nature fairies in Ireland say the same," agreed Lana.

Choekyi nodded, deep in thought.

"But this is a modern world," said Kai. "How can we go backwards?"

The old woman sighed. "It's following circles... So somehow it's bound to come back to a beginning... The ancient stories tell of dolphins giving signs of the dawning of a new era...of peace and love... And all the kids working towards it."

"Oh?"

"And one of the signs is the appearance of a dolphin boy."

"Oh!"

"It's said, he's to have an enlarged head at the front...like the ancients."

18
Poisoned

That evening, they all sat down in the hostel dining room to a sumptuous meal of taro, beans and fries with papaya. "You should've seen the waves!" said Tane, excited at the huge swell he and Hank had been surfing. The others had watched open-mouthed with respect at the force of the ocean – gigantic barrels to dream of.

"I wasn't going to risk going in," said Josee, about to shovel in a mouthful of food when she suddenly stopped, sniffed and put her fork down. "Actually, I'm not going to risk these fries either. They don't smell right to me." The others all laughed at her and continued eating.

"You've been working with too many drug barons!" joked Lana. Josee nodded. But a little while later, as vast quantities of ice cream were being eaten, it was Lana who was doubled up with tummy pain and looking green, closely followed by Moz and then Choekyi and then Tane. One by one everyone clutched tummies and dragged themselves away to vomit.

"We'll investigate," said Mr Dung, looking intensely nauseous himself. "It looks like food poisoning. Security, please could you have a word with the kitchen staff for us?" But Security's usually stern face was in a twisted grin and he merely shook his head and rushed outside.

"I'll do it," said Josee, and returned a few minutes later.

"Everyone else in the hostel seems okay. It's just us," she reported. "But it's weird. One of the staff said they'd just found a note scribbled across the orders list saying, 'yellow-bellied sea snake'."

Mr Dung groaned and collapsed onto the floor.

"They've ordered an ambulance," she said as she grabbed a cushion for his head, trying to keep out of the way of bright orange vomit projecting onto the floor in a stinky gooey slime.

Kai staggered outside and was sick all over the white hibiscus bush, just missing the hostel cat. He was no stranger to vomiting, but it was scary that his brain sent messages to his arms and legs which didn't respond properly. His muscles just stiffened up. Somehow he crawled to his bed, dragged on pyjamas, and curled up, trying to hold the cramps in his tummy. His eyes were heavy and he wanted to sleep, but he was too restless, searching desperately… There was a Phinny-sized hole around him. He clutched uselessly at it. Where was Phinny? If only he could sleep… He missed Mum and his dog, Bandit. And wished he was home…

He must have lost consciousness because the next thing he was aware of was a sharp pain in his arm, a bright light and a kindly face in a green uniform leaning over him. "Hold still, young man. You're going to be okay. We're giving you the anti-venom. Luckily we were alerted to yellow-bellied sea snake poisoning, so we've been able to do a vomit test and administer the antidote quickly. Everyone will be as right as rain soon. Just rest, please." Then everything fell into an uneasy darkness.

The next thing he knew there was sunlight caressing the ceiling and a familiar voice was whispering to him. "Kai… Kai, look. I've found a friend of yours." Josee's face was peering over him, pressing a finger to her lips, and she was holding a crumpled but beloved Phinny. Kai reached up his arms.

The hole that had been filled with loss was suddenly filled with joy. And he fell into a contented sleep.

"Kai, we're here now. Be ready for adventure."

Kerploosh!

A double tail fin crashes down on the surface of the ocean, making a lot of noise and creating a fabulous fountain of water. Kai realises he's wearing pyjamas which are now drenched and soggy, but he doesn't care. He's with Phinn.

"Turnin' turtles! Can't you dress properly for your dreams!"

"How am I meant to do that?"

"You have to imagine yourself into a suitable outfit."

"Okay… Um… I'm a super-hero king-of-the-ocean…" In a flash, Kai finds himself wearing a horned helmet, brandishing a sword above his head dripping with seaweed, swishing it this way and that, keeping at bay an army of aggressive yellow-bellied sea snakes.

"Wow, it works!"

"Of course it works. It's time you learnt anything works in dreams. But better not be antagonistic towards the sea snakes."

"Well, we were nearly all poisoned..."

"Dumpin' dogfish! You have to work to connect with things, not be against them."

There's a huge explosion of light and Kai blinks with the brightness. Arcing above him is the magnificent white body of the Snow Dolphin, mesmerising eyes holding his.

"We want you to know," she says, "that because we are all interconnected, things will only be in balance if we all work together with love for the good of everything."

Then the vision is gone, as though it's never been there in the first place. Kai shakes his head. Has he imagined it?

"Turnin' turtles! It was me that imagined it and brought the Snow Dolphin for you."

"Phinn, how could you imagine something so...so awesome?"

"I'm supercool."

"Oh, sorry. How could I forget!"

Phinn kerplooshes down with his tail fin again. But Kai is still puzzling about it as he wipes water from his face.

"How come we're all interconnected?"

"Well, just think...You're dependent on everything around you – the sun, the soil, the air for life... You can't live in isolation."

"I guess..."

"It's true... Nothing is separate."

"Okay. What do I do then? Say: Hello, lovely sea snakes. Love you."

"Yes, exactly that!"

"No! That's silly."

"Try it."

"Okay. Here goes: Hello, lovely sea snakes. Love you."

He sees sea snakes – black on top, bright yellow underneath, with blotchy tails. They circle round in the shape of a heart. Kai swears there're smiles on their faces. Then they happily drift off in search of fish eggs for dinner.

"See?"

"Why do you always have to be right?"

"I'm supercool."

"Thought you'd got rid of your ego, Degbert..." Kai splashes down on the water with his sword trying to soak Phinn, but only manages a pathetic little plop.

Phinn giggles with high-pitched squeals.

"Next time I'm going to imagine myself with a huge shield," says Kai.

"C'mon, let's see if we can create sea rainbows..."

"Isn't that impossible?"

"I keep telling you – in dreams nothing is impossible."

"You're impossible, Phinn." Kai tries to playfully whack the dolphin, who kerplooshes loudly and dives out of reach.

He awoke to an afternoon downpour pounding on the tin roof with rainbows dancing on the ceiling.

Thankfully he felt normal again and was able to join the others relaxing on the veranda drinking a recovery tea made from local leaves. He sat next to the hibiscus, now a rather pretty shade of orange. He wasn't surprised that the discussion was of the poisoning.

"Strange that no other groups in the hostel were affected," said Mr Dung, now looking himself again under his cowboy hat. I'm afraid someone is trying to target us."

"But how would anyone even get the venom?"

"Security has talked to the police, who found traces of poison in the fries' oil, but they say that yellow-bellied sea snake venom is often collected here for medical research as a blood anticoagulant. So it's not easy to track. And there's not much more they can do."

"Unless someone is used to snakes..." murmured Wilga, looking at Moz.

"But there isn't anyone..."

"Well, you're a snake-charmer, Moz, aren't you?" Wilga said.

"How d'you know that?" he said, glancing sideways.

"I link with Aboriginal rock spirits...little mimis...connecting me to the Earth," she replied. "They show me pictures in my mind. When we were all relaxing and singing the other night I saw a picture of you in a desert land, swaying back and forth together with a snake in a basket. There were people throwing coins."

"But I wouldn't... "

"No, nor would Josee, but she wouldn't eat the fries that everyone else had," said Bibi.

"But, I never would—" said Josee, looking upset.

"Neither Tane, but he said his Pacific culture considers sea snakes as gods to be revered, so we should make the most of their gifts..." said Victa accusingly.

"That's ridiculous," said Tane forcefully.

"Winning race cheating isn't winning race," pointed out Choekyi. "Some very keen to win." He looked at nobody in particular, but it was Hank who squirmed.

"Yeah, but not enough to stop everyone else winning the race..."

"Well, what about you Russians, Victa?" said Lana, fiddling with her red plaited hair. "I saw on social media you are genetically creating new types of snakes altogether, and maybe venom..."

Victa threw her a dirty look and strode away.

"Careful Lana," Kai whispered. "It could be a knife she throws next time."

"Now, let's not get carried away," said Mr Dung. "I'm sure we can all talk about things properly with each other. Then everything will be great, as we'll have trust. I really believe you young people can show adults that it's quite possible to have trust between nations."

Well, thought Kai, there doesn't seem to be much trust between the kids at the moment. He thought of the Snow Dolphin's understanding about everything being interconnected and working together for the good of all.

How to reach that state?

It appeared that Mr Dung believed it possible.

However Mr Dung was sighing and Kai wasn't the only one who heard him mumble, "But it certainly seems someone doesn't want us to do this race."

19
Crystal Jigsaw Piece

Dratbag!

I sure don't want to do this race, thought Kai a few days later, as he stopped running and bent over, gasping for air. It was his first taste of running high on the mountain – with a monster oxygen-sucking slime blob clinging to his chest restricting his breathing. It would've been scary – if Mr Dung hadn't warned that the lack of oxygen would make them feel weird. And that, with time at altitude, their bodies would acclimatise by producing more red blood cells.

They were trying to run up the steep slope to the White Mountain Visitors Centre at 2,800 metres. It was diabolical, but Kai noticed it was the running that made breathing super hard. When he gave up and moved slowly, his breathing eased back to normal.

They'd had time to recover from the food poisoning. Everyone had put it behind them and settled down to the routine training of running along the coast trails. Kai's bruises were disappearing, and he and Moz had an uneasy truce, with Moz glaring at him and Kai trying to keep out of his way.

Now Security sat smugly in the driving seat of the minibus, still wearing his suit, having dropped them off for the short run, saying, "Have fun, delinquents."

Tane scoffed, "I'd like to see you try this, Security."

"Someone's gotta keep an eye on you," Security replied, nastily. The kids reckoned he'd been watching too many movies and liked to swagger about like an important bodyguard.

He drove slowly up behind them, gradually picking up those who had decided that the torture of running while barely able to breathe wasn't worth the effort and had given up. Only Bibi, Victa and Hank made it all the way, puffing and panting like grumbling adults.

Mr Dung greeted them at the information building with a big smile on his face, standing beside displays of unique flora and fauna which included a white stone statue of a dolphin. "Gee! Well done y'all! Now you know what it's like running at altitude without acclimatisation."

There was serious nodding.

"Tough eh? Kids younger than thirteen aren't even allowed higher than here. But bodies are clever, and with loads of water and time to adapt to the low oxygen, you'll be okay. So we'll spend time here today to get the process started."

Kai was half listening – more interested in the dolphin statue, and watching Victa approach with a strong, "Haa", sending life-force through her palms to the dolphins. He'd seen her do this before with other large mammal statues, to send strength to those species, but was pleased to see her respect here for the dolphins. Her focus was absolute, even after the effort of running. It was always surprising that the statues didn't disintegrate into a thousand pieces!

He then looked beyond the buildings at the alpine desert that rose imposingly above them in shades of beige and brown. It was so huge the summit wasn't visible from where they were – just round cinder cones where lava had burst out, perched pimple-like along the skyline. He felt like he was in a video game, with the sense that lava would pounce out and get him at any moment.

"It's not pointy like a volcano should look," he said.

"White Mountain's a shield volcano," said Mr Dung. "Layers of slow lava made it very wide. It's dormant, like a waiting watchful warrior, not likely to erupt for another few thousand years. Unlike its active neighbour..."

They all stared in awe.

"There's someone special here who wants to meet you kids," continued Mr Dung, as a man in a dark green uniform approached. "This is the Ranger. He's the guardian of the mountain."

The man had long silver hair pulled back in a ponytail, showing a striking Hawaiian tattoo swirling down the right side of his face. He was small in stature but with a powerful presence – the presence of a watchful warrior, just like the mountain. He went round greeting everyone with a casual Hawaiian handshake, slapping hands followed by a finger hug. Tane and Hank seemed familiar with it. But it gave Lana the giggles. And both Moz and Bibi were so embarrassed they just stared hard at the ground.

When it came to Kai's turn, he felt awkward,

sure he was going to mess up, but as he looked into deep quiet eyes there was a flash of recognition. He gasped. It was like looking into the eyes of the Snow Dolphin, seeing all knowledge of the past and future, shining brightly. Strangely, it gave him the feeling that he was going to run up this mountain for the dolphins.

Kai flicked his head, not sure what he'd just experienced.

"Aloha… Welcome to White Mountain," the Ranger spoke warmly. "It's good what you do. To come with purpose. This has long been sacred land for our people – the place that connects Mother Earth to Father Sky." He looked to the far distant sea. "And just as our ancestors navigated their canoes to these islands by the stars, so today the stars are used to navigate into the future, both from the astronomical observatories constructed here and the inner observatories within our minds."

Kai stared enthralled as the Ranger explained, "The top of White Mountain is the place where the modern telescopes of high-tech science sit next to the powerful burial grounds of our native Hawaiian kings."

A flash of sadness crossed the Ranger's face as he added, "Though many have no understanding of this… But we have ho'oponopono."

The kids looking at him questioningly.

"Ho'oponopono is our powerful Hawaiian way that brings harmony. It translates as, 'I'm sorry, please forgive me, thank you, I love you.'"

He stared upwards to where a hiking trail led into the clouds now rolling in, covering the mountain like a blanket.

"So, I ask that you connect to our mountain with love. And respect our culture. Please neither remove nor leave anything."

"Please, Mr Ranger..." It was Choekyi, who spoke quietly, "Request. May we leave gift?" He rummaged in his pocket and held something out in his hand for the Ranger to take."

It looked like a long piece of cut glass. Six sides glinting. Pointed both ends. It was translucent quartz. "Tibetan peace crystal. From my country in Himalayas. For compassion. Gentle wisdom."

The Ranger held the crystal in his left hand and stared at it for what seemed like minutes, while Choekyi stood quietly by. Then the tattooed face burst into a smile. "Mahalo, thank you. It's an honour that you bring something precious from your culture to ours... From your heart to ours. This is how the world will come together."

He held his right hand over it. "I'm adding the blessings of Hawaiian aloha magic to give you all strength for the run. You may place it on the altar at our sacred summit. We rarely give permission to climb to this final section of the peak. But you children may climb. You bring hope."

"Thank you," said Choekyi, placing his hands together on his heart and bowing slightly.

"But," said the Ranger holding the crystal up to the mountain, confirming it to be an offering of immense value, "I have a request too. Not far below the summit is a magical green lake. Scientists have no idea why it holds water. For as long as Hawaiians have talked story, the chiefs have placed the afterbirth of their babies in this lake to bring strength for their lives... My request is that you dip this crystal in the lake. It will then carry peaceful strength, not only for you runners, but for all children, to the sacred summit of White Mountain...for the birth of the new golden era."

There was silence in the minibus on the way back down. Until Hank said, "It's weird – that putting babies' afterbirth in the lake."

"I think it's rather beautiful," said Wilga.

"Well," said Mr Dung, "Not so strange when you know it's common on every continent across the planet. Even the Brits used to do the same thing."

"Really?" said Lana.

"Yeah... They used to bury afterbirth under oak trees to bring strength for babies' lives."

"Well, that's Brits for you," said Bibi, looking at Kai…

Kai wasn't really listening. He was still under the spell of the Ranger, sure he sensed a feeling of deep calm, like that of a jigsaw piece correctly placed.

But there were many pieces of the jigsaw still missing.

And turmoil to come before it could be completed.

20
Call of the Conch Shell

Kai puzzled over the link between the dolphins and the Hawaiian people, both with a similar mystical force about them. Why did it feel so important? Dolphins live in Hawaii, yes, but also in many other parts of the world. So what was it? After supper that evening in the hostel, having pretending to listen to Mr Dung go on and on about the experience of running at altitude, and Security drone on about keeping their room tidy, he realised who would know the answer.

He knew his link with the dolphins was Phinny, so he quietly collected his soft toy and tucked him into his trousers underneath his t-shirt.

"I'm going down to the bay," he informed Mr Dung, who was now making endless lists about kit.

Moz had already gone out, Tane and Hank were involved in an argument about who was the best surfer. Victa was practising her martial arts with shouts of "Haa!" which had the hostel cat fired up in defence mode – back arched and scruffy hair on end. Josee and Bibi were trying on running clothes, each insisting they needed to look their best when winning the prize.

"Want to come?" Kai asked Choekyi, who was looking left out.

He shook his head. "I go meditate. Connect with stillness. Practise peacefulness."

That's why he's always quiet, thought Kai.

"Wait," said Lana. "I'm coming too."

"Me too," said Wilga.

"I want to see if the Kahuna is there," Kai told them.

Sure enough, they arrived at the little beach just as a pink glow was spreading peacefully across the ocean, beside the grey crest of the world's tallest mountain. A full moon was rising to the west. Frogs were chirping and waves lapped harmoniously, but they were suddenly drowned out by a long mournful call. They stared.

At the ocean's edge stood a small figure, long skirt floating in the water, lei around her neck blowing gently in the breeze. Her head was tipped back to the sky. She held to her mouth a huge conch shell, from which the call was coming. Rich and strong. The sound reverberated across the evening calm like a drum.

The Kahuna.

"Aloha, Dolphin Boy," she said without looking round, as though she'd been expecting him.

"How did you know we were here?"

"The conch horn called you," she said, turning and holding up the beautiful shell. "Good magic..."

She bent to pick up leis that were resting on the sand and placed them around their necks.

"Lets dance hula," she said, hips starting to sway back and forth with arms out and hands expressing the directions of the waves and the flights of the diving seabirds. The girls joined in, giggling as though this was a natural thing they'd been doing all their lives, but Kai felt self-conscious and unsure, until dragged laughing by the others into their ring. Soon, as the Kahuna started chanting mesmerising words, he relaxed into the rhythm and shut his eyes, feeling just the movement of the sound, the sand between his toes and the joy in his heart.

Then a funny thing happened.

One minute he was there dancing back and forth on the beach. The next he felt all disjointed and was lying asleep on the sand.

"We're here now," says a familiar voice.

They're in the gentle swell of the ocean flowing back and forth, amid the shining river of silver spewing from a bright full moon. The light is catching the underbody of a breaching flash of dolphin.

"Phinn! What're you doing here?"

"Supercool dancing with you of course!"

"Fishbrain!"

"Pleased to see you too... Listen, the Snow Dolphin wants to show you something. The dolphins want you to understand what life was like in the time of Mu."

"The time of the ancients...?"

There's a blazing splash of dazzling light. Swoosh! And they're joined by the glistening Snow Dolphin, surrounding them with fine mist, like a cloud from a waterfall.

Then the mist vanishes to reveal a group of see-through people with huge beating hearts, clearly visible. Their hearts seem to control everything – from finding food, to building shelters, to communicating. It's all done through heart energy.

Kai can tell that the see-through people are happy and peaceful and having fun.

Then, just as suddenly, the picture is gone and he's looking into the infinitely wise eyes of the Snow Dolphin.

"The land sank below the waves, leaving only the tips of the mountains," she says. "This is now the islands of Hawaii, the last remnants of a wonderful land."

"Why did the land sink?"

"The people couldn't maintain their heart-centred ways. This led to disaster."

"Ooh!"

"But before they went, all their knowledge of the old ways of living in harmony was given to the dolphins, who promised to hold it until needed again."

There's an ocean commotion as a vast pod of brother and sister dolphins appear behind her, with great kerplooshing all around, singing "Now is the time..."

There's more loud kerplooshing.

"Yes, now is the time to receive the knowledge, so humans can move into the new golden era."

With each kerploosh, Kai experiences a cold whoosh, like a giant shiver, up and down his back.

"Take action!"

Kerploosh! Whoosh!

Louder and louder…

"Wake up!"

"Wake up, Dolphin Boy," the Kahuna was shaking him. "You were shouting."

Kai sat up in a daze.

He told her what the dolphins had said. "It was amazing. Everything was created with heart thoughts…"

"Ah," she said, nodding thoughtfully, "the energy of aloha…of love. This is the ancient tool, used by the Hawaiian people, but to be used now by everyone for the golden era. Carry it with you…"

Wilga smiled excitedly. "My mimi guide showed me a picture too… Of hearts beating with the same rhythm."

"And I heard the nature fairies singing and dancing with us," beamed Lana. "So cool!"

The Kahuna nodded, not surprised at their awareness. "Return with all the kids at dawn before the race and we'll make more Hawaiian magic." She threw them an aloha hand sign, middle fingers curled, thumb and pinkie extended. Then she drifted away.

The girls helped Kai stand up, slipping their arms into his, one each side, as they headed off back from the beach. His heart was lighter. Just for a moment he felt the true support of friends.

They passed through shadows held back from the moonlight by the bushes. "Hey, shh!" said Wilga suddenly, finger to her lips. "There's someone there." They peeped through the foliage at a tiny sea inlet and saw a shadowy figure on the rocks, bending over the dark ocean. The figure had hands almost in the water, but a head swaying slowly back and forth… Too slow to be hula.

"What's going on?" said Lana.

"Sh!" whispered Wilga. "I think it's Moz… Look, the cap's back to front, so it must be him."

"Probably catching sea snakes," said Kai. "C'mon. Let's go." He was fearful of Moz and didn't want to be spotted spying on him. He suddenly felt shaky and the mosquitos were beginning to bite. Then he was startled by the dark shape of a bat fluttering by, using its sonar to hunt down a juicy meal. He hurried on towards the light of the hostel.

Fear has a habit of swallowing up confidence.

It was to get a whole lot worse.

21
Test of Strength

"We must remember we're on the world's most active volcano," said Mr Dung, cowboy hat all askew with enthusiasm. "So, melted rock at 1,400 degrees centigrade waiting just below the surface to pour out – which it does from time to time."

He spoke to the kids as they clambered out of the minibus at the road-head, ready for the training hike on Long Mountain.

"Will it explode?" asked Lana, wide-eyed.

"Hope so," said Hank. "Can't wait to tell my friends I've been on a live volcano!"

Even Choekyi seemed excited.

"Well," went on Mr Dung. "If lava does pour out, it should be slow and steady – we wouldn't have got a permit if there'd been a high risk today. So, it's great we have one, as it's crucial we hike up Long Mountain, which offers the only opportunity to sleep two nights at altitude, to prepare our bodies for the race up White Mountain."

Kai was nervous. This was a proper big expedition and they'd been talking about it and preparing for days.

Mr Dung had been a hiking guide in his young days, so had been passing on knowledge of stuff like map reading, mountain safety and how to pee in a blizzard.

And Security had caused a stir that morning by appearing without his suit, in heavy boots, shorts and t-shirt, showing off his paunch. The kids had cheered loudly at the change.

"Ooh look, it's Thor from Marvel," said Tane.

"No, it's Dumbledore from Harry Potter," said Wilga, making everyone laugh.

Security had growled, squirming uncomfortably, "Right, you delinquents, let's have some discipline here."

By the time they'd driven into the Volcanos National Park and Security had ducked into the park office to get the permits, Kai knew this cap-over-bald-head version of Security wasn't any different from the suited one. The same vibe of dislike was there, so Kai still kept a safe distance from him.

Kai's negative thoughts had persisted, as the minibus bumped along the road through thick forest in pouring rain, carrying them as high as possible. He knew he wasn't trusted by most of the group…wouldn't speak up for himself…was scared of being shouted down… And he was anxious about just being on the mountain, not wanting to make a fool of himself…

But as he climbed down from the minibus he resolved: 'this hike is to prepare for the race… I'm sure I can do this…and my dreams confirm it'. At least he'd managed to sneak a certain dolphin into his rucksack. Phinny didn't weigh very much, though Kai had no idea how hard he'd find climbing all day with a heavy load.

They each had tough walking boots and a large rucksack, ready for two nights at the cabins on the mountain. The rucksacks were bulging with kit: sleeping bag, warm jacket, waterproofs, map and compass, head torch, food and – heaviest of all – their allocated three litres of water. Mr Dung and Security also had stoves and fuel.

"A ridiculous weight to carry," complained Josee as they shouldered the packs.

"One thing we agree on," said Moz.

"You'll soon get used to it," said Mr Dung. "But it's important we go slow and steady. No race today. I'm confident you'll be great… You're all fit and determined. And, gee…this acclimatisation may decide the outcome of the race itself."

He glanced over at Bibi, still in the minibus, fiddling with the silicone gel liner of the walking leg she was using today, aware there was still a feeling of resentment over her running blade, which could help her win the race.

Security was shouting at her crossly, "C'mon, get a move on."

"You try living with one leg," she retorted, making a rude face.

Mr Dung put his pack down. "While we're waiting, let's do something important the native Hawaiians do. We need to show respect to Pele, the goddess of fire, who lives in the volcano."

"Just legend, isn't it?" said Hank.

"Yeah, but gee… She represents the natural world here, and humans have been so disrespectful to it, anything we do to redress the balance is good." With that Mr Dung held his hands up to the sky and became lost in thought.

"I heard she pretends to be an old woman begging for a drink of water and if you don't take pity on her she'll send hot lava and burn your house down," Hank laughed.

He hadn't seen that Mr Dung had tears in his eyes, saying, "Great Pele, we thank you for allowing us on your mountain. We come in peace!"

Kai thought Mr Dung's actions were strange, but felt pleased they were respecting the local traditions of the land.

Bibi picked up a stick from beneath the trees to steady herself, ready to set off.

Within ten minutes they were plodding up the track which opened dramatically out from the jungly forest onto scrub land, where swathes of black, brown and red lava crisscrossed their path. The rain had stopped and they could see the way ahead marked with piles of lava stones known as ahus.

It wasn't easy crossing the lava. Some was like lumpy cowpat, some like jagged, bashed chocolate. All of it was awkward and uncomfortable to walk on, particularly uphill with a heavy load. The sun now shone down relentlessly. And already there was a fierce wind blowing, which brought with it the volcanic sulphur smell of rotten eggs. This upset Josee, who covered her nose with a scarf, saying, "Bad sign."

"Can't win race with weak nose," sneered Victa. The kids' banter was all about who was fastest – and indeed toughest – in these conditions.

It certainly wasn't Security. The long root of a bush did the dirty and tipped him up. One minute he was plodding along. The next there was a thump, followed by a squawk like a strangled chicken. Kai turned to see him rolling on the ground, clutching his ankle.

"C'mon, get a move on!" someone shouted.

Mr Dung tried to help him up.

Security shook his head. "I'm sorry… Twisted my ankle and can't go on. Have to hobble back to the minibus and head back to the hostel. You lot go on. I'll come back for you the day after tomorrow."

"Can you drive?" asked Mr Dung, concerned.

"Yes, yes. It's my left foot. The bus is automatic. I'll be fine."

"What a bummer! Let's keep in phone contact anyway. Oh, and give us your stove and first-aid bag."

So it was decided. And Victa picked up the extra kit saying, "No problem. Life-force makes me tough."

They plodded on steadily upwards, Kai making sure he was last, so didn't have to talk to anyone. Anyway he had to concentrate on placing each foot carefully so the weight on his back didn't unbalance him, until it became more a part of him and he relaxed. He felt a bit like the turtle in the sea carrying all his needs, which gave him strength.

He could see Victa, Hank and Tane leading the way with seemingly endless strength. Then Moz, Wilga, Lana and Choekyi, chatting with Mr Dung. And Bibi and Josee following, deep in conversation.

They stopped every so often to drink and catch their breath, as they gradually rose higher above the clouds. Then a lone tree dripping with red flowers provided shade for a stop to sit and take packs off, while Lana appeared to chat with the tree. They looked back and saw Long Mountain's main side crater belching smoke below them, wafting the strong smell of rotten eggs into the air.

"Doesn't feel right," said Josee, looking more concerned and pulling her scarf tighter around her nose.

"Explosive force!" said Victa excitedly.

"That's Puu Oo..." said Mr Dung. "It's often active."

"Good name for a pooing volcano," said Lana.

"Well..." said Mr Dung, "the Hawaiian alphabet's only twelve letters, so they make the most of the ones they've got."

"Even so, Puu Oo doesn't seem real," said Tane.

"It's Pele acknowledging us," laughed Hank, looking at Mr Dung.

Certainly it confirmed they were on a live volcano.

Just then, a little brown lizard approached Bibi cautiously, eyeballing her briefly and then scurrying off in a hurry.

"A dragon friend of yours?" asked Wilga.

"The guardian spirit the Hawaiians call Mo'o," nodded Bibi quietly so no-one else would hear.

"Hmm… Looks like he knows something we don't," said Wilga as they gathered their rucksacks and headed onwards and upwards.

The trudging became relentless. Kai had never had to walk for so long without taking rests. He longed for a nice cold drink… Then his thoughts were imagining a bounding Bandit dog beside him, making him feel sad. He so missed his canine friend… His boots rubbed his heels. Straps burnt his shoulders. Pack weight felt like ten Bandit dogs. But at least his sweat was rapidly eaten by the fierce wind.

After three hours there were dark lava tubes, like skateboard half-pipes, with tunnels and deep cracks revealing frightening holes. And an eerie temporary feeling, as though the crumbly spent lava beneath their feet had stopped in mid flow, frozen in time.

Everyone became more and more subdued as the day wore on, climbing higher and higher, with just a few spiky shrubs to look at, too tired to complain about the struggle and the weariness. But then, wonderfully, a little red cabin appeared.

It had a red corrugated metal roof and painted wooden walls, with a shady verandah around the front and a tiny building alongside for a loo – a shack a long way from anywhere, but heaven.

It'd been a gruelling and exhausting six hours. But at least they were now above 3,000 metres. Kai dumped his pack along with everyone else's on the verandah, threw his boots off and collapsed on one of the bunks inside. I'm never going to be able to move again, he thought.

Mr Dung busied himself boiling water on the stoves. He didn't like the dead-mouse look of the water collected off the roof into a barrel, so used the precious supplies they'd carried. It wasn't long before everyone had a meal from the dried packets stirred up, which were surprisingly edible. Kai was feeling too sick and tired to eat but Mr Dung insisted, and soon he felt a bit better.

Whilst the water was boiling for hot chocolates, Kai went outside and wandered a little way, pleased he'd carried flip-flops and didn't have to put boots back on his sore feet. The temperature had dropped considerably. The smell of rotten eggs had subsided. The sun was disappearing below the horizon in a blaze of orange and there were stripes of colour across the sky. But all he could see was a huge presence over to the north. The race mountain! – a vast half-dome rising into the heavens, standing proud above an ocean of cloud. He felt profoundly connected to it.

"Hello White Mountain," he whispered.

The reply was an extraordinary sound. Total silence. Wow! Kai felt something beautiful touch him deep inside.

The moment stayed with him while he slurped a drink, dragged an exhausted body up to a top bunk, snuggled into a sleeping bag with Phinny and closed his eyes. He really hoped he wouldn't have busy dreams…

22
The Sea Unicorn

A jolly voice is saying, "We're here now... Be ready for adventure."

Kai groans, "I'm tired, Phinn... Go away! It's been

a tough day."

"When things get tough, look at the big reason behind what you do."

"Go away. I want to sleep."

"You are asleep. C'mon... I'll take you on a journey and remind you why..."

"No! no more..."

"Dumpin' dogfish! This is a dream! Tell you what, let's get you a dolphin body for a bit... Then we can swim the seas fast and have more fun than in that pathetic human body. You've already got the large forehead. That'll help."

"Phinn... I can't..."

"Stop complaining. Now... I want you to think yourself into a dolphin body – the most streamlined beautiful being there is... Imagine your body is even better than mine..."

Kai laughs and relaxes and imagines... Whooopeeee!!

"Supercool!"

Suddenly, as if by magic, he's a torpedo of joy and energy, hurtling through the water alongside Phinn... Then leaping and twisting and flying and diving like he's been been doing it all his life.

"Phinn, this is amazing!" he shouts in his mind.

"Told you it was the best..."

Maybe he could even try...the giddying turn of a somersault... He lifts his flippers up and pulls down quickly as he curls and rolls his streamlined body. "It's...it's so free... Whooeeee!!" He breaches and flies and dives deep, with no fear. Only joy in his veins... He's part of the ocean... He is the ocean...

But it's an ocean of sound. He's seeing by sonar. The world is vibrational soup. His range has become vast... From birds in the sky above to tiny plants and all-sized fishes in the sea, there's high-pitched life going on everywhere. He focuses down to nearby clicks and whistles, sending them out from his large forehead, and receives them back via his jaw into his inner ear. His body tingles with thrilling sensations. It's nothing – absolutely nothing – like he's ever experienced or imagined before... A whole new world of wonderment...

Suddenly his joy is interrupted. He hears a piercing screech like a train going through a tunnel, blocking out all other sounds. It hurts his inner ear. He looks to Phinn, "What's that?"

"Ship engine... It disrupts dolphin life far and wide," Phinn says sadly, coming alongside, tail softly rubbing, still communicating mind to mind without speaking. "C'mon. There's someone we've got to meet."

He leads off north in the direction of the magnetic pull towards the polar vortex. On and on over endless seas...

They seem to travel a considerable distance timelessly, accompanied by a blur of warm currents, until Kai is aware that a temperature change has happened. Things are getting cooler.

He's keeping close to Phinn, when suddenly he senses fear. They'd been speeding along, but his sonar detects a wall ahead…coming fast.

"Stop!" Phinn yells.

They rise to the surface for breath-time and Kai gasps in surprise. They've come up alongside a huge white iceberg mountain, which tips back and forth. Most unstable. Above it the sky is silver-grey and heavy.

Away to the side there is choppy, inky-blue sea, littered with small ice floes. On one there's a mother polar bear looking forlorn as her two weary cubs cling to her desperately in fear, as the floe is splitting. He can feel their terror.

On another a crying mother walrus is trying to give birth to her baby, but is tipped into the ocean by the floe breaking up. The mother is frantic.

But Kai's attention is drawn to the other side of Phinn, who's shrieking, "An ocean commotion!" accompanied by squawking sea birds. He sees in horror that there's an army bearing down on them. An army of huge mottled grey beings with long single tusks. Narwhals! Their sound travels ahead of them, a loud high-pitched mass-clicking that screeches like a human warship.

"Don't be afraid," says Phinn.

"Understatement…"

"Extend your heart-light around yourself... Be steady..."

"What...?"

Kai tries hard but doesn't know what he's doing and is too scared... The beings are coming closer at a tremendous rate. He wonders in a flash, how do they manage such speed without dorsal fins. But no time to think further. They're upon him and Phinn. He feels numb. In a time warp.

"Phinn, I can't do it.. "

He's being pushed and shoved... No, he realises, I'm being played with... I'm going to be eaten.

"Phinn... Help!"

That's when he feels a warm glow around him, which somehow he knows is Phinn's heart-light encircling them both, and feels Phinn's body alongside his flipper. He realises he hasn't released the breath he's holding – a waiting-to-be-attacked-and-eaten breath. Now it comes out in a rush, "Wheeeoooooo!" A long breath of relief.

"Steady... Hold steady, Kai."

Phinn turns and calls to their attackers, "We come in peace... We bring fish-light from the sunlit isles. We mean no harm. We'll not upset your hunt."

There's a gnashing of tails and a great snapping of water by the long tusks.

"Please... We wish to speak with the Sea Unicorn. Is she here?"

"She might be here...and then again she might not be," says one huge narwhal, who eyes them piercingly, as though they are a delicacy on his dinner menu.

Kai quakes with a shiver of fear which sends ripples out beyond the protective heart-light.

"Steady," whispers Phinn. "Hold love in your heart-light..."

Kai lets out another deep breath and shuts his eyes and tries to concentrate on love... Hard... Very hard... He concentrates on the love he feels for Phinn, and holds the feeling as though his life depends on it, which, he thinks grimly, it does...

"Supercool," encourages Phinn. "Now make it bigger. Send it out."

Slowly he expands the love outwards as though he's blowing up a balloon, until he feels it cover the pack of fierce narwhals and they're surrounded by a warm glow. Only then does he dare open his eyes. The pack seems to have calmed a little and is now swimming slowly around Phinn and Kai in circles...

"We need to speak to the Sea Unicorn urgently... It's a matter of great importance to help Earth. We have to stop the ice melting."

This seems to calm them further and they swirl, facing each other with their long tusks clashing, conferring. Then one slighter female peels off and heads behind the swaying ice mountain, clicking rhythmical messages, a straight clean swell piercing the water behind her.

"Supercool! They're getting the Sea Unicorn," whispers Phinn. "Now remember, don't look her in the eye. Show respect."

Cloud formations gather and the silver sky turns to mercury white as a huge wave arrives, rocking all the waiting bodies. And a whinnying screech, which brings all the threatening narwhal beings to an unnatural silence.

A beautiful glistening white narwhal appears from behind the iceberg and moves elegantly and effortlessly towards them, long corkscrew tusk shining brightly. Kai knows he couldn't look the Sea Unicorn in the eye even if he wants to.

He tries to copy Phinn, who is bowing his head slowly up and down and moving gently backwards.

"Welcome, brother dolphins," she says, voice like liquid sunshine. "My sister, the Snow Dolphin, said she would send you, to see the destruction of the northern magnetic vortex... Similar to the loss of mountain snow crystals in her sunlit isles. The natural order of life is broken here in our beautiful wilderness. Our glaciers are retreating, spewing bergs off to disappear. The ice we have relied on for generations is gone. Our animal populations are out of balance and disappearing. All because of the melting ice..."

Kai listens intently.

"Our young are suffering. They are crying out as food sources dry up. Our brother land animals...the polar bears, the walruses... They also will do anything for their young, but without the ice they have nowhere to go. Their homes are vanishing. They are dying."

She lifts her elegant tusk from the water, which drips from it like tears.

"Our brother penguins in the south magnetic vortex are experiencing the same. Their homes on the ice-shelves are calving off. Their communities are being decimated."

There's an agonising whistle from Phinn. Kai senses his anxiety, remembering he's had a previous assignment as a penguin. And reaches out a flipper to him in a touch of understanding. Phinn becomes calmer.

The Sea Unicorn continues, "The problems are due to the human activities which are disrespectful to Earth, and causing temperatures to rise rapidly, melting the ice."

Oh no, thinks Kai. Whatever can we do?

The reply comes, "My sister the Snow Dolphin and I agree that the human species should take responsibility. So, if the human young rise up, then, as with the animals, the adults will listen and do what is needed."

The Sea Unicorn waves her beautiful tusk with a flourish, like an enchanted wand, and her body glows brighter and brighter until she disappears from view.

Kai can just hear, "We must prepare the humans for the golden era. It is coming."

And fainter still, "The human young must rise up..."

But, he wonders, can the kids make that difference in time?

"Yes indeed, Young Human," echoes back. "Kids bring hope..."

23
Tears in the Sky

Kai woke to bright dawn sunlight shining through the little window beside his bunk. It was cold. He put on all the clothes he had, still in a daze from the intensity of the dream.

Mr Dung was boiling water for breakfast. "Rise and shine, guys!"

Rise and shine… Hmm, thought Kai, the Sea

Unicorn's words still dancing in his head. How do you rise up? What is the golden era? What does it all mean? He mulled it over while gathering his kit and eating his packet of dried porridge with strawberry jam. At least the other kids were quiet and subdued. It was six in the morning after all.

"We have a full day's hike ahead and 1,000 metres to climb, but we must get to the summit cabin before nightfall," said Mr Dung. "And we need to hike slowly to give our bodies the best chance of acclimatising to the altitude. If anyone suffers badly then we all must go down. Best to stick together, as there's no other adult. Nor, it seems, any mobile phone reception."

"We so miss Security," said Bibi sarcastically and everyone laughed, getting the day off to a good start.

Various blisters and sore spots were plastered up and they set off at a steady pace, amid groans and complaints about the still heavy loads and sore feet.

White Mountain looked stunning beside them, rising out of a bed of clouds into a clear ocean-blue sky. It was a reminder of the challenging race to come and what they would have to put up with that day on Long Mountain to get acclimatised so it would all be possible.

To begin with, there were no problems – just a steady plod upwards across the volcanic wilderness, everyone determined not to be the one to slow the group down or – worse – to cause them all to turn around.

Kai chatted to Lana, who was finding breathing tough and seemed to be worrying about something. "What's up?" he asked.

"It's the nature fairies," she said between breaths. "They're unsettled. They think something big is about to happen."

"Like what?"

"Don't know. I couldn't work it out."

"Probably about to be pooed on by a nene goose. Apparently they used to be over a metre tall. I'd be worried about poo from that-sized bird."

Lana smiled. "But look, there's no birds around. Don't you think that's strange? I'm more worried about being pooed on by a volcano. And that makes me frazzled."

"My dream guide says, when things get tough, look at the big reason behind what you do," Kai said, and giggled.

Lana shrugged. "Get acclimatised… Win race… Do something good for nature fairies. Right now, too stressed to care."

Kai continued to try and cheer her up. "Look at all the cool colours of the lava… There's black crunchy cowpat with icing sugar and sharp bashed chocolate. And fields of tomato sauce, brown gravy bowls and even golden honey dollops…"

"Thanks Egghead, but that's making me feel queasy..."

As the day wore on and they climbed higher, Kai developed a stonking headache, which shut him up. But they were not the only ones to suffer.

Wilga started wheezing, much to her annoyance.

Both Bibi and Tane were struggling to breathe and kept having to stop to catch their breath.

Victa, Moz and Hank were keeping ahead, and disguising any headaches and dizziness well.

Choekyi, acclimatised from living at altitude, but physically not as strong as the others, struggled with the heavy weight on his back.

Mr Dung himself was going super-slow. He'd taken medical advice on whether to give the youngsters the standard altitude-sickness medicine but was advised against it, so decided not to use it himself in solidarity. But he handed out painkillers to those who requested them. He wanted to say, "drink lots of water," but didn't know what the water situation was at the summit cabin, so told everyone to be sparing with their drink.

Only Josee seemed to be okay. She trudged up, happily chatting to everyone, chewing away at something. Eventually she confided in Wilga, "I'm chewing coca leaves from home in Colombia. They help with the altitude by slowing its nasty effects."

Hank overheard and said loudly, "Taking an illicit drug is an unfair advantage on the race."

"It's part of my culture," Josee insisted.

"Well you're not in your country now. And I'm saying it's illegal."

"You're just jealous 'cos you haven't got any."

By then they all knew about it and stared daggers at her. Kai wasn't quite sure what to make of it. Everyone, he thought, had some sort of unfair advantage in their own way. He could be told off for having long legs.

Mr Dung said nothing, lost deep in his own thoughts.

Morning had moved into afternoon by the time they came up to a fork in the trail on the rim of the summit crater. They were so tired they barely bothered to look into the huge cauldron. They slumped down gratefully onto the rough ground to rest from the slog. The altitude was now over 4,000 metres above sea level.

There was no respite from the sun's heat, the relentless wind and the struggle to breathe. And here the smell of sulphur was even stronger…

"Yuk! Smells like your farts," Moz said to Kai, keeping up his meanness in spite of being exhausted.

Kai ignored him, dropped his pack and lay flat on the rough ground. He was feeling intensely nauseous. His head was pounding and spinning. The blisters on his heels were agony. And he wished he'd never come on this silly adventure.

"We'll have ten minutes break here," said Mr Dung, trying hard to appear normal, but his words came out in gasps. "The actual summit is over there." He waved his hand across the enormous bowl filled with jet black lava, riddled with ominous spirts of steam. "But we'll head round the rim in the other direction for two miles to the summit cabin."

No one took much notice as he wandered over to the edge of the crater, which dropped 200 metres straight down to its base. Kai idly watched him take something yellow out of his rucksack, wrap it round a rock and hurl it hard into the depth of the vast steaming hole.

Kai was intrigued. He dragged himself up and staggered over to the edge where Mr Dung was sitting, cowboy hat off, head in hands, and sat down beside him. He was horrified to see that Mr Dung was sobbing. "Oh… I didn't mean to disturb…"

Mr Dung looked up and smiled through tearful eyes. "No…it's okay. Thank you." He put a hand on Kai's shoulder. "I owe you an explanation. You see…" He paused to gather himself. "I had a son. He would've been your age now. But…but he died in a wild fire… Extreme weather conditions caused by climate change." He paused again, staring far into the distance. "That's why I chose thirteen-year-olds for this race. And that's why I want to make a difference for the Natural World Crisis. So that he didn't die in vain."

Mr Dung sighed heavily and wiped a tear from his cheek, adding, "I couldn't save him..." He rolled up his sleeve and showed Kai leathery burn marks on his forearm. "I would've given my life for his...but I couldn't save him."

There was a long silence.

"I'm so sorry," said Kai. "I didn't know..." and hung his head, embarrassed to see Mr Dung's grief.

"So I was just making an offering to Pele, goddess of fire, to show respect... I threw my son's cap into the crater... P'raps foolish, but it felt meaningful to me."

Kai didn't know what to say, so said nothing. But he could somehow sense Mr Dung's pain inside his own heart. Maybe, he thought, that's his heart-light I'm seeing...

After a few minutes it came to him. "Mr Dung... We'll do the run...for your son... It will make a difference. He won't have died in vain."

"Thanks Kai. That means the world to me."

Kai felt a surge of energy enter his tired body. Perhaps this wasn't such a silly adventure after all.

By the end of the afternoon, everyone had made it to the summit cabin, close to the side of the crater, in varying states of altitude sickness. It was just a corrugated metal box, painted steel green, but never had civilisation seemed so welcome. There were bunks, three-tiered along the wall, and shelter from the elements, especially from the now very cold wind. Most of all, it was shelter from the struggle.

Exhausted, dizzy and nauseous, the kids helped with the jobs – sleeping bags to put on mattresses, stoves to light, water to boil, packets of food to stir, though no one could face eating. And hot chocolate to make.

The water collected in a barrel off the roof looked like cat-sick, so Kai joined Lana to follow 'waterhole' signs. Dusk was falling as they made their way to the edge of the crater and carefully climbed down a little crack to a ledge. The exposure didn't bother Lana, being a rock climber in Ireland, but Kai was nervous and his arms and legs were shaking. Normally he wouldn't have risked going near a steep drop to oblivion, but the group was desperate to drink more to ease the dehydration from the hiking and the altitude.

His foot skidded, knocking rocks which bounded and fell into the seemingly bottomless pit. He held his breath and met eyes with Lana. She just nodded. Relieved on reaching the ledge, he found a puddle of ice. Oh no! They would never be able to cut it to fill their water bottles. Then Kai spotted a little meltwater pool beneath it in a hole, and, by hanging upside down, managed to scoop up some precious liquid and hand it back up to Lana to pour into the other bottle. Eventually they had one and a half litres, and scrambled back up out of the crater.

On the way back to the cabin they stopped at the loo. The sort that might win a 'scariest loo' competition. It was two sheets of metal leaning against each other over a crack which dropped 200 metres down to the crater floor. Luckily their bodies were too dehydrated to need it, though Lana thought it'd be fun to try. Kai had had enough perching on the edge for one night. Besides he was shivering violently – whether from altitude or fear he wasn't quite sure.

They reached the cabin just as the sun was setting, surrounded by gathering clouds. The cold was now biting like a thousand knives. The sulphur smell was strong. They were in the arms of Long Mountain. Or, he thought as he lay down to sleep, were they perhaps in the arms of Goddess Pele?

He's not sure if he's actually asleep, but there's a lot of noise going on… There's repeated banging and rumbling…and shaking…

"Kai!"

"Go away, Phinn."

"Kai!"

"Leave me alone…"

"Wake up!"

There's kerplooshing.

"Take action!"

He reached out to find Phinny and opened half an eye to retrieve his soft toy and pull him into his sleeping bag….though he had to push the covers away as he was too hot… But…hang on… Something didn't feel right.

There was an orange glow to everything. He could feel dust on his fingers. There was a dull grinding sound. And the air was heavy with the smell of sulphur.

What was going on?

He opened the other eye. The gaping door was banging back and forth, fed by a strange wind. But what he saw on the other side of the door, where there should have been a purple starlit night, made him sit bolt upright in horror.

The sky was on fire!

24
Pele Wakes

Kai kicked his legs over the side of the bunk. Fell to the floor, still in his sleeping bag. Wriggled out and ran to the door. Grabbing his boots, he forced them on and rushed outside. He was hit by a wall of heat. He gawped. The scene that greeted him was like something out of a Star Wars video game.

A firestorm was roaring out of the crater,

throwing exploding flaming gasses high into the night. It cast long dancing shadows onto a low canopy of cloud. Rocks were raining down amid swirling ash which the wind was buffeting around in circles, whipping up every bit of loose lava in its path. The ground was trembling as though gathering energy to pounce.

Kai squatted to steady himself and put his hand on the ground. It was hot! At that moment he saw a burning rock land on the wooden window ledge of the cabin and fire up, instantly devouring the flimsy curtains inside, before moving onto the timber lining.

A grumbling noise was getting louder and louder. He put his hands to his ears as if to confirm it wasn't really happening… As if…

"Wake up everyone!" he screamed. "The volcano's erupting!" His words were taken by the wind which was conducting an orchestra of catastrophic sound.

He tore back into the cabin, which was now shaking with a deafening roar of rock bombs landing on the roof. There was chaos. Everyone was in a daze, frantically trying to rouse themselves. Tane was coughing uncontrollably. Choekyi was standing open-mouthed. Moz and Hank were shoving things into rucksacks. Victa was shouting, "Boots!" and grabbing the first two she could find, then throwing them off and scrambling with everyone to find ones that fitted, before running outside.

Mr Dung was lying in his bunk staring wide-eyed at the flames taking hold on the roof. He wasn't moving. Kai shouted at Lana, "Help me!" And together they hauled him up, shoved boots at him and pushed him, staggering, outside and away to a little island of higher ground where the others had gathered. There they forced his boots on him.

"Are we all out?" yelled Hank.

"Where's Bibi?" Josee shouted in alarm.

The cabin did a violent shudder and tipped scarily sideways. At that moment Bibi appeared in the doorway, false leg in hand. Her face was contorted in horror at the gap to the ground – too far to jump, even with two legs. She shouted something that sounded like "Mo'o!" as the blaze close behind licked her hair. There was a violent booming explosion. Fire, shooting sparks and smoke, erupted on all sides. She screamed and fell forward. The clouds of ash appeared to blend into a long face with red-hot eyes, a body with a large pointed tail that swished back and forth and wings that carried her down, through the chaos and confusion. Tane and Hank stared, gobsmacked, then rushed over, grabbed her under the arms and dragged her like a puppet across swaying, crumbling rock, pulling her onto the higher ground. Here Wilga and Lana held her steady while Josee, fumbling in panic, helped her tug her leg on.

But terror awaited.

"Oh My God!" yelled Moz, pointing towards the crater.

A river of blazing orange lava, tinged with scarlet, came creeping over the horizon, the rim of the crater. A vast living thing leaking blood. It pushed old black rock before it like a wave on an ocean. Slowly advancing. Closer and closer. Mesmerising.

Suddenly there was an earsplitting roar and a huge fissure appeared, into which poured vast quantities of the black lava which made up what was once ground. The cabin swayed drunkenly and proceeded to slide down into the bowels of the earth, after which came immeasurable tons of what had until minutes before been solid rock.

The kids stared through the dark, now lit by lurid bands of shining red, at where the cabin had been, moments before. Where they had all been. It was hard to take in. There was just a gaping hole, now fed by a landslide of dark loose lava, rolling over and over in a thunderous rumble.

Everyone seemed too stunned to move. Then Wilga and Lana started crying. Bibi, Josee, Moz and Tane took to swearing – words that any footballer would be proud of. Choekyi was reciting mantras. And Mr Dung stood in shock like a statue of an elfin gargoyle. Minutes went by.

It was Hank who gathered his senses first and shouted, "We've gotta get outa here fast!" But his shriek was gruff and strange – his great grandfather was speaking through him, trying to help.

"Now to eternity! Pau ole!" he screamed. Then rambled on in an old language that no one understood or took any notice of.

Kai let out the breath he'd been holding. But it didn't seem to stop his whole body shaking. He studied his feet, not knowing why, but pleased he'd found his own boots coming out of the cabin. That thought died as another thought came in. Raising his head he observed where the cabin had been, now buried somewhere deep in the earth. It was as though he wasn't the one thinking the awful thought...that now, buried somewhere deep in the earth with it, was his beloved Phinny. And that meant...that meant...all his dream contact with Phinn was cut. He wouldn't be able to speak with Phinn any more. No more diving and spinning nor kerplooshing...

Hot tears burnt his eyes. Claws grabbed him sharply around the heart.

He heard a scream, "Egghead!" and turned...

Everyone was confused and scrambling away from the fissure and the river of burning lava. The higher ground where they were couldn't possibly be safe for long. But which way?

Nobody got far. They stopped and gathered together. At least they could now hear each other speak.

"We must follow the trail," said Victa, pushing ash from her face. "The ahu piles of stones show us the way."

"No way," said Moz. "That way is close to the crater for two miles. It could burst again anywhere any moment."

"Straight downhill is sensible," said Josee. "We'll eventually end up at the sea somewhere."

"No, that's miles of wilderness," insisted Tane, coughing. "We'd never make it."

"Has anyone got a map?" asked Wilga.

The two with rucksacks, Moz and Hank, shook their heads.

"What about water or food?" asked Bibi.

Moz delved into his pack. "Half a bottle of water and a smelly cheese sandwich," he reported.

Hank offered, "Most of a bottle and a couple of energy bars and some pre-chewed chewing gum. But look, I have a head torch." He was back to sounding like himself, as though he hadn't noticed the appearance of his great grandfather.

"Have to risk trail," said Choekyi quietly. "Only chance in dark."

At that moment there was a tremendous roar and the sky was lit up by a huge fountain of fire-red molten rock from within the crater. Silhouetted against it was the hunched figure of Mr Dung, not moving.

"We can't leave him," sniffed Lana, thinking about someone else to help her feel calmer.

Hank and Tane clambered back up and spoke to him, but returned, shaking their heads. "He won't respond. It's as though he's not there."

"I'll try," said Kai.

"What good could you do?" spat Victa.

Kai felt resentment from the group. But he had to try.

He calmed his racing heart, banging head and dry mouth just enough to retrace the steps to the higher ground. Taking the man's hands he looked into his stoned eyes and shouted, "He didn't die in vain, Mr Dung!"

There was a flicker. A shake of the head. And a squeeze of the hand.

"Mr Dung. We have to go. We need you."

Mr Dung nodded as though suddenly awake. Took a couple of deep breaths of gas-ridden air. Coughed. Shook his head and looked around, taking stock. And together they staggered back to the others.

"Up to the trail, now." He spoke as though there wasn't a volcano erupting over them. "Look for the first ahu. It's just up there."

Anyone got a head torch?" He looked around.

"Right, Hank, when you get to the ahu, shine it

so everyone can see. Then when everyone's there we'll search for the next one and do the same all along the trail."

They spread out, back up towards the crater but away from the fissure.

"Here it is," shouted Josee.

Then they followed the trail along the crater edge, lit by Pele's fireworks, and tried not to look into the huge bubbling cauldron alongside them. A burning pit. From ahu to ahu they made their way, slowly but steadily, Lana and Wilga helping Bibi, who was struggling with her leg, until they came to the sign at the fork in the trail.

Turning they could see the lava river two miles behind them, following its deadly course downhill. Thankfully, they turned away from the crater and headed steeply downhill in a different direction, on the long trail towards the first cabin. It got darker and darker as they went, and harder and harder to find the ahu – painstakingly slow, but what a relief to be moving away from the noise and the spirting flames. And now they could breathe slightly easier. And though their throats were dry and raw, at least they knew that every step downhill would bring more oxygen to their lungs.

But the fire goddess had not finished with them. They were spread out, searching for the ahu near an old cinder cone around which the trail was winding when there was an almighty earsplitting crash. The old crusty lava trembled beneath their feet. A hot wind raced over them.

Kai looked up, sensing rather than seeing the ground crack above him and a high wall of red hot lava rolling inexorably down towards him. Its centre was bright orange and it dragged crimson red and gave birth to black at the edges. From the middle, spirts of fire shot out, illuminating this new river of relentless power and majesty. A new fissure was born.

Kai stood motionless, opening his eyes wide and holding his hand to his mouth in horror. Then terror surged through his veins. He turned and ran. In blind panic he ran downhill, twisting and turning, trying to sense the flattest way across uneven and sharp ground which tipped him in all directions, not caring where he went. Just away. Anywhere but there. He could barely see what he trod on, and fell repeatedly onto his hands, harsh lava tearing into his palms. Excruciating pain shot up his arms. But the pain merely spurred him on. Running… Running…

After a while, the panic eased. His mouth was so dry his lips were cracked and bleeding…legs like jelly…no breath left…lungs spent. He stopped and doubled over, gasping again and again. Then fell painfully to his knees. I can't go any further, he told himself. This is it. I'm finished.

Noticing he'd stopped alongside a deep black

shadow, he put his hand out and felt a gap in the ground. He stretched his arm and felt further. More space. Standing up, he moved further still, down into something… The gap continued until he realised he was in some sort of cave. He could feel a wall. He moved along it, hand over hand. It seemed to go on and on. There was stillness. It was completely dark. I wonder if this is one of those lava tubes, he thought. It was enough for him. He slid down to the bottom, curled up in a ball and rocked himself back and forth, crying like a baby.

Moz is right, he thought. I am a baby. I can't do strong. The lava can cover me up. I can't move any more. I've had it. I can't even dream any more. I'm no good.

And he closed his eyes.

25
Gift of Courage

"Kai!" Someone was calling his name. It echoed as though coming from a long way down a tunnel.

"Go away!"

"Kai!"

"Leave me alone!"

"Kai! Are you there?"

The ocean shouldn't be this hot. Why is it hot?

He opened his eyes. There was light. He wasn't dreaming, but he must have been asleep. He could see a dimly lit black wall. He blinked and turned to the source of light. He was in a tunnel, a hot tunnel.

He could see a circle of light at the end of it, with a figure standing in the middle.

"Here!" he tried to shout but his throat was so dry it came out as a hoarse whisper.

The figure turned away.

Kai tried to get up but his legs were so stiff, he couldn't move. His hands felt weird, covered in something dark and sticky. Blood. Oh no, caked blood.

"Here!" he tried again, but nothing came out.

The figure had gone.

No!!

He painfully wiped the floor with his fingers, found a rock and threw it at the wall opposite as hard as he could. The sound echoed back along the tunnel.

The figure returned, paused and then started walking in his direction. Footsteps resounded loudly. "Kai! Where are you?"

He threw another stone.

More footsteps.

Strong arms reached out to him.

He found himself being hauled up and helped hobbling down the tunnel until he was hit by the blinding light of day.

There was a smiley Mr Dung.

"I've found you," he said. "Everyone reckoned you'd been eaten by the lava. But I wasn't going to give up on you."

"Sorry," said Kai, noticing that Mr Dung was looking extremely dishevelled and limping badly, and even his precious cowboy hat was full of holes and burn marks.

"It's okay. Look, I want to show you something. Turn around."

Kai turned and looked back up the mountain. Barely a hundred metres away was a gigantic black wall rising at least ten metres high, scattered with spots of burning fire-red.

Confused, he turned back.

"It's the end of the lava river," said Mr Dung. "It's in its cooling phase now. The lava is solidifying rapidly around it, creating a crust. Don't you see?" he beamed. "It stopped just above you. Pele spared you."

As if in confirmation, there was a shrill call from the sky just above. Peering up they could see a magnificent bird of prey soaring gracefully.

"He's hunting those running from the lava," said Mr Dung. "But, gee... Look... See the beautiful fan of his tail. I think it must be one of those rare Hawaiian hawks that the Ranger was talking about. He said they're royal birds that bring courage."

Kai was dimly aware of being touched by Hawaiian magic, just when he needed it.

They hobbled back to the red cabin, where the other kids were asleep. They'd all kept ahead of the lava river and, still following the ahus, had managed to find the cabin in the early morning. Luckily a team of vulcanologists was there to study the new eruption and had been able to give everyone food and drink with the aid of water purification tablets. And some first aid to all the burns and bruises. Amazingly, no one had been seriously hurt.

The vulcanologists had been surprised to see them. They had understood that all public permits had been refused for the last few days because of the expected lava flows. So how had Security obtained them?

After a short rest for Mr Dung and Kai, they kindly helped everyone back to the road-head. It was only a four-hour walk downhill with no weight to carry, but everyone was completely drained from exhaustion, lack of food, dehydration and battling the altitude. And fear and trauma had taken its toll too. No one had the energy to talk.

Security was meant to meet them at the road-head with the minibus. But there was no sign of him. So, with phone signals back on, Mr Dung was able to borrow a mobile and speak to him.

"He'll be up as soon as poss to pick us up," said Mr Dung. "Strange, though. He sounded surprised that we were all back safely."

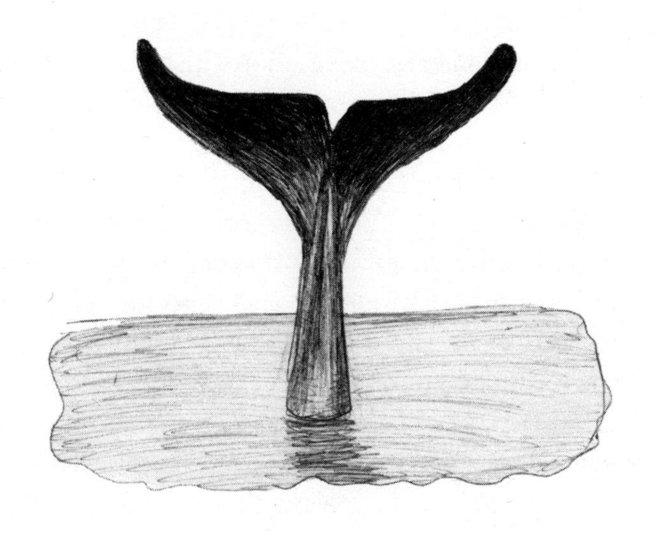

26
What Makes You Strong

Kai didn't care that all the boys would hear him crying. They all knew he was a cry-baby now, so what did it matter? He curled up in his bed that night at the hostel, trying to sleep. But even though he was more worn out than he'd ever been, he couldn't sleep.

He was too tired to pretend that he didn't miss

Phinny, now gone forever. Anyway, the others were all coping with their own exhaustion and recovery.

After a while he seemed to just run out of tears. He lay thinking, and all his thoughts of the experience on Long Mountain played through his mind – the difficulties, the fear, the pain… But at least he'd survived. Which is more than Mr Dung's son had. Which got him thinking: 'Mr Dung's standing up and keeping going without his son. So, surely I can stand up and keep going without Phinny. Maybe I don't need him any more. Maybe I can let him go'. There was something about that thought that gave him a surge of energy inside… A sort of high, free feeling that he quite liked. Hmm…

It wasn't long after this that Kai heard one of the others get up and rummage about and come and stand beside his bed. It was Moz. He looked almost sad, as though he didn't have the energy to be unkind any more. He threw something down in front of Kai saying, "Here's your stupid teddy."

Kai sat up. He couldn't believe his ears. Nor his eyes. For there beside him lay a bedraggled, well-adventured soft toy. Phinny.

"How ever…?"

"I picked him up at the top cabin…in the rush on the way out…off the floor…"

"Oh wow!" It pained Kai to say it, but he was

unbelievably grateful to Moz. "Thank you."

Never had sleep come so sweetly.

"Kai! We're here now. Be ready for adventure."

Phinn is spy-hopping on calm blue water. They're in the middle of an abundant happy ocean. Bright sunlight is shining off a shoal of flying fish chased by dive-bombing gulls and sea-terns. Brother and sister dolphins are playing alongside, leaping and spinning.

Kai tries to hug Phinn, but his nose gets swamped by a nifty sideways move of a tail fluke and a kerploosh which knocks him underwater in a double rollover somersault as though he's dream-flying. He comes up for air, coughing and spluttering and laughing.

"Phinn! I thought I'd lost you."

"Turnin' turtles! You're not going to get rid of me that easily."

Phinn kerplooshes again and Kai laughs and lies on his back floating, looking up at the clear sky, feeling deeply happy.

"Watch out for supercool bird poo in your eyes. You humans don't have jelly tears like we superior dolphins do." Another kerploosh comes.

"Oy!"

"So, tell me how're you enjoying the experiences of being on an adventure, puny human brother?"

Wow, thinks Kai. Phinn called me 'brother', which makes me feel all warm inside… Though he's a fishbrain for calling me 'puny'!

"Puny Loony!" sings Phinn. "Remember I can hear your thoughts and see your heart-light. You can't pretend anything with me. C'mon tell me… How's the adventuring going?"

"Well, to be honest it's been really tough."

"Dumpin' dogfish! You do know, don't you?"

"What?"

"Going through tough stuff makes you strong."

27
Dynamite Day

Kai's hands were mending fast, though he'd probably end up with scars – battle scars like Moz's face perhaps…

Tane, Wilga and Mr Dung still had sore feet after the delay in putting boots on at the cabin, but daily dips in the sea, good food and light running were helping recovery and a return to health and fitness. And the local medic who'd checked them over had declared them all good to go.

Mr Dung was happy to see that the inner resilience that he'd picked the kids for was indeed there and that they'd all bounced back from such a traumatic training hike, but it was good that he'd included a big chunk of rest time in the programme before the impending race-day.

Security had apologised that he'd made a mistake with the permits and yes, they shouldn't have been on Long Mountain. And what a shame they'd nearly been killed by the volcano. But his ankle was still so bad he needed to spend a lot of time in his room.

"Sulking," said Bibi.

"More like feeling guilty," said Josee.

"No, I think it's highly suspicious," said Hank. "And we need to watch him carefully."

Mr Dung had little time to talk things through with the kids. He was busy with the logistics for the race and dealing with all the local government bodies to make sure it would go smoothly.

So it was Security who was to take them on the day's outing planned, as part of the rest and recovery time, to the north of the island. He was to take them in the minibus and wait while they climbed down a long steep track to a beach and then, after an explore, clambered back up again. This would give them some exercise to keep their muscles ticking over. And they'd see a beautiful valley, once home to the old kings of Hawaii, before the islands were taken over by the US. It was considered a special valley by the native Hawaiians, although since it was destroyed by a devastating tsunami in the middle of the last century, it was no longer much visited.

They arrived and parked at a magnificent viewpoint at the top of the cliff. There was no one else around. A deserted, wide, black sandy beach spread before them, cut by a little river that slipped into bubbling white surf. The valley was guarded by 800-metre steep cliffs that gathered waterfalls and tumbled down into lush tropical vegetation. It wasn't difficult to imagine ancient kings living in this paradise.

"You've got three hours," said Security, straightening the jacket of his suit. "Don't be late. Leave lots of time for the way up. It's a killer. Ha ha!" He limped over and removed a rope across an unstable looking track that led steeply over the edge and disappeared from view. The kids weren't bothered by steepness – even Bibi with her walking leg on – and happily started clambering down.

After a minute or so, Kai remembered he'd left his gloves in the minibus. He'd promised the medic he'd wear them for this tricky scramble. "Dratbag!" he said to Lana. "Sorry, I've gotta go and get them."

He climbed back up the steep slope, but coming to the edge, he stopped. He could hear Security speaking on the phone. He listened.

"No, it'll be easy. Dynamite's ready. I've researched a good spot where minimal blow will cause most damage... What?... No, not a chance anyone'll survive. Entirely natural. Unstable. Always slips on this trail... Yes, this time I'll definitely get them."

Kai put his hand to his mouth, trying to work out what it meant. Moving quietly to the side of the track, he peered through thick vegetation at Security swaggering as he spoke into the phone. "I nicked an old box of sticks from the military base that no one'll miss. Ha ha!"

That was when Kai noticed... Security was walking without a limp. Kai's heart missed a beat as he realised what this might mean. Surely not? Could he be wrong? Yes... But equally, he could be right. Then he remembered the strange way Security had said, "Leave lots of time for the way up. It's a killer. Ha ha." Kai felt himself go cold, as if a cloud had covered the sun. He had to get back to the others.

Holding a deep breath he turned as quietly as he could and scuttled carefully back down. They hadn't gone too far and were sitting discussing the merits of tsunamis.

When he reached them he couldn't say

anything. He became tongue-tied and his heart was beating hard in his chest. Eventually he said, "Listen... You've got to listen." "Why should we listen to you?" said Bibi, and everyone laughed.

He still couldn't get it out. But Lana said to the others, "We must listen guys. I've a feeling this is important. The nature fairies have been trying to warn me about something... Listen..."

And then it came pouring out. "It's Security. I heard him on the phone. He's about to blow this track with dynamite. Start a landslide. He wants to kill us all."

"Don't be ridiculous," said Bibi.

"Why'd he do that?" said Josee.

"You can't expect us to believe you, surely?" said Victa. "We don't trust you."

"Kai's right," said Moz quietly, and they all turned to look at him. "I've been watching Security for a while. It was him that poisoned us all. I'm sure. It's just that I don't have proof."

"That's bonkers," said Tane. "Why?"

"I've no idea," said Moz. "But we need to find out."

"His heart not warm," said Choekyi.

"You mean we have to trust Kai?" said Victa.

"Not sure I can do that," said Bibi.

"We must believe him," said Wilga, firmly. "The rock spirits, my mimis, sent a picture of a landslide. I thought it was the volcano. But now I can see it's this valley."

Kai took a deep breath, trying to be strong. "And…I saw Security walking fine – without a limp."

"That settles it for me," said Hank. "I think we should split up and double-back through the undergrowth, so that at least we can see what he's up to."

Stealthily, the kids crept back up through the vegetation out of sight. Then, as if someone had given a signal, they all walked into the clearing together, surrounding Security. He was standing next to the open door of the minibus, holding a small wooden box of dynamite sticks.

There was no mistaking…

They walked in closer.

"What d'you delinquents want?" Security said angrily.

"We want to know what you've got there," said Hank, pointing at the box.

"Cigars," said Security.

"Don't be stupid. I know dynamite. It smells of bananas," said Bibi. "We use it in the mines in South Africa."

"Smells of scum," confirmed Josee.

"What if it is?" Security said, glaring threateningly at Bibi.

"You snotbag! You were going to set off a

landslide, weren't you? With us in the way."

"Yes, maybe I was," Security sneered. "Now, I'm going to have to finish you off in a different way. But your bodies will still be buried under a convenient landslide." He put his hand into the pocket of his suit.

"Watch out. He's got a gun," shouted Wilga.

Moz was coming in closer. Scar down his face. Mean look in his eye. Knife drawn in front of him… "You were the one who poisoned us all, weren't you?"

"What a clever little boy you are," Security sneered as he pulled a revolver out and pointed it at Moz. "How did you know?"

Moz spat back, "I know snakes. They communicated your energy to me as I connected to them at the sea edge – an unnatural energy that indicated stealing their poison for negative effects. I couldn't get more, but I knew."

Security's hand wavered on the trigger.

"I was the one who left the yellow-bellied note in the kitchen," Moz said, trying to keep him talking. "And you were the one who sabotaged the plane and arranged for Hank's father's car to be vandalised."

"What a shame I'll have to kill such a clever little detective," Security said, keeping his eye on Moz's knife. "And don't forget the volcano. Who was it that forged the permits to get you all onto the live volcano?"

"You're going to know what it's like to be disadvantaged," snarled Bibi. "Just wait!"

He turned the gun on her and then back to Moz. "Don't you delinquents want to know why?" he asked. "You should know before I kill you all." He turned the gun in a semi circle so each one would know what it's like facing a gun.

Nobody said anything.

"Well, I'm going to tell you. It's for money. Lovely lovely money. Big oil companies are paying me a fortune to stop you doing the race, so you don't disrupt their fossil fuel industry by making a silly fuss about the Natural World Crisis. They want to stay rich. I'm going to join them."

There was an angry growl from Tane, who surged forward, shouting, "Greedy scum! You're causing sea level to rise. And my country's disappearing below the waves."

Security turned the gun on Tane and squeezed the trigger.

"Akahele!" shouted Hank in a gruff great grandfather voice that left no doubt it meant, "Watch Out!"

Kai, next to Tane, without thinking, stuck a long leg out in a perfect football move and Tane fell heavily to the ground, just as a bullet sped over his head, singeing his hair.

Moz ran at Security, knife closing in, just as

the shot went off. But before he could reach him there was a swift bear-like strike from the side and a body flew in with a Russian cry of "Haa!" and in one lightning movement Victa had delivered Security a devastating blow in the head with the side of a foot.

Security fell backwards onto the minibus. The box of dynamite sticks he'd carefully been holding in his hand shot off and landed hard against the far inside door.

The world seemed to pause…then Bibi shouted, "GeDown!!"as an explosion ripped through the vehicle, throwing door, seat, roof, wheel hub, wing mirror, metal and shattered glass into the air.

Kai threw himself to the ground. Or maybe the blast did it. He never really knew. And buried his head beneath his hands, waiting.

There was a clatter as bits of bus came to earth.

Then silence.

Was he still alive?

Was anyone else still alive? He lifted his head.

There was a lot of smoke. And moving bodies. Phew!

He watched as Victa rushed up to the body of Security, which was twitching, and chopped sharply on the back of his neck with her hand. Then Security lay still. She bowed gracefully as though completing a martial arts tournament, murmuring, "Hmm… Good to practise that move."

Tentatively removing the gun from his hand she placed it well out of his reach. "Very strong life-force," she said. "Unconscious for a while." Then slid her hands up and down in good riddance.

Slowly everybody got up and dusted themselves down.

"Everyone okay?" asked Lana.

"Let's grab his phone," said Hank, back to modern voice, rummaging in Security's pocket. "Must be some good evidence there." He pulled it out and tossed it to Josee.

She scrolled through, "Yes, He's been phoning a couple of international numbers a lot recently. Ah, here's Mr Dung's number." She put it onto loud speaker as it rang.

Mr Dung answered, "Hello Security. Please phone later. I'm busy."

"No it's Josee here, Mr Dung."

"Oh, is it something important?"

"Yes, well…you see…"

"Josee, out with it. I'm in a meeting…"

She looked around at the remains of the bus, "Mr Dung, I think we might have accidentally blown up the minibus."

"Oh my goodness! Are you okay? Where's Security? Can you put me onto him?"

She looked at the body Lana was rolling over, practising climbing knots, tying arms and legs neatly together with the rope from across the track. "Well, actually he's a bit indisposed. But it would be useful if you could phone the police for us."

Lana surveyed her handiwork – a suited man nicely trussed up – and decided, "This'll earn me the Girl Scout rope-skills badge."

Choekyi's thoughts were of Security's actions. "Him long karma," he said, shaking his head.

For Tane, as he wiped the gravel and dust from his face and turned to Kai, shakily picking himself up, it was, "Thanks man. I owe you."

Kai, remembering the time Tane had helped him in the canoe on the sea, said, "It was nothing. I'm stronger than you and used to the land." And they both laughed.

Hmm, thought Kai. Did I really say that? He had a feeling that helping someone else had made him feel better about himself. Could that be the strength that Phinn was talking about? Was he feeling stronger inside?

When Security had been taken off to jail and the excitement had died down, Kai was left feeling rather stunned at yet more extreme danger. All the other kids were a bit subdued for a while too. There was a lingering sense of trauma.

Hmm... he thought, maybe it takes a little time to adapt to tough stuff making you strong.

But trauma aside, the time was fast approaching that would test his inner strength to the limit.

Race day!

Things were hotting up...

28
Claws Out

The minibus hire people were not amused. "Our slogan, 'Love You To Pieces', is meant to refer to the beauty of our island, not the state you return our vehicles in," they said. "And no, we will not give you a replacement on the grounds that the last one fell to bits."

This gave an opportunity for others to

volunteer help, showing the wonderful aloha spirit. Mr Dung was inundated with kind offers of support vehicles for the race, and accepted a jeep and an ice-cream truck.

And the exploding minibus produced media-frenzy headlines like, 'Kids blow corporation sky-high', so everyone now knew about the kids from around the globe running up the tallest mountain to help the Natural World Crisis.

"Gee, this publicity is great!" said Mr Dung. "Good always comes out of bad. So let's ask as many kids as we can to write us peace messages – pledges to help peace for the natural world – encouraging them to make a positive difference, with love for the Earth... Young people power to be expressed from the mountain! I've already emailed your schools in your home countries and they're sending in messages. Awesome!"

Kai liked the idea of peace messages but wasn't too keen on celebrity status. It made him feel uncomfortable.

But most of the kids thought it fun, and a way to show they were the best.

"Brill!" said Hank, proudly. My handsome face on screens and advertising deals."

"See Russian champion," boasted Victa. "Good propaganda."

"A disadvantaged girl showing how to win," said Bibi.

All this increased the rivalry between them. They watched each other warily, closely comparing training times.

Mr Dung inadvertently encouraged the rivalry by organising a live TV show, so each competitor could tell the world what they'd do with the prize money. This created more rifts between them, each vying to be more important than the others, and seemingly trashing the trust that had been beginning to build up between them. Kai didn't like the way it made him feel isolated. He'd felt happier when everyone was doing stuff together.

He anxiously watched the preparations for the show. The hostel dining room had a table with microphones and lights at one end and a film crew at the other, and was to be introduced by a big-nosed presenter sent over from the US. He was dressed smartly in Hawaiian flowery shirt and plain white tie, so he could look suave and sophisticated, as befits a top presenter.

Everyone involved was awarded a colourful flower lei so there would be no doubt they were on the paradise islands of Hawaii. Though Moz refused to wear one on the grounds of being African, adding, "They make you look girlie."

The presenter preened about in front of a mirror, held up for him so he could check his false hairpiece wasn't askew and his bulbous nose wasn't shiny. He stood behind the table, notes in front of him. Cameras focused in position. They were ready to begin.

"Right! Let's roll, guys! Remember to look at the camera with the red light on." He turned towards it with a wide grin, not unlike an orangutan being tickled.

"Five, four, three, two, one...action!"

"Good evening folks in the US and around the world. Welcome to a world premier contest! We're exclusively bringing you the story of kids, from all continents of the planet, who're about to tackle something impossible. That is, impossible for you or me, viewers... It's a run, yes, a run, up the world's tallest mountain, here on the Big Island of Hawaii. We'll be bringing you the epic race itself in two days' time. Tonight the children will tell us what they'd like to do with the considerable prize money they're fighting for. Also, we've asked them to answer the tantalising question, 'what would you like to say to adults about the Natural World Crisis?'" He paused for effect... "It all happens here, folks."

He waved in the first contestant. "And bravely starting us off is...Josee from Colombia!"

She skipped in looking sweet and childlike, ponytail bobbing, in a skirt and FNZ t-shirt, announcing, "I'm going to win the money so I can help my village pay off the drug barons."

"Cut!" shouted someone from the back of the

room. "You can't say that!" There was a moment of confusion and the presenter's nose grew red with frustration.

"Eh..." he hastened on. "Well, baby doll, what would you like to say to adults?"

"That life's about helping people, not making money – you really don't have to be rich to make a difference."

"Viewers may disagree there, but thank you," the presenter said, quickly waving Josee on. "So our next competitor is Hank, from our very own USA. Yeah!"

Hank swaggered in looking charming and confident. "I'm gonna win this and buy the biggest best electric car you've ever seen."

"Great," said the presenter, relieved at the sensible answer. "And what about your message to adults, Hank?"

"Grow up and stop polluting the planet!"

"Okay. Thank you. Now...here we have our representative from South Africa. It's Bibi!"

She came in, shaking her afro fire-singed hair and sat at the table, making a big show of her false leg to gain sympathy. The presenter certainly looked like he felt sorry for her, asking gently, "Tell us how would you spend the money, little girl?"

"I'll build a house where I can feel safe."

"Oh! Really..." He didn't dare ask 'why?'. "And your message to adults?"

She stood up and spoke angrily. "You've stuffed up! You've taken too much from our world. Give it back, or I'll set my dragons on you!"

"Right… Okay…" The presenter tried not to look ruffled, twiddling his chin as though he'd just swallowed a jellyfish. "Er…thank you… Next we have our competitor from the Pacific Islands of Kiribati. It's Tane!"

He walked in purposefully, looking tanned and attractive in his flowery shirt. "I'll spend the prize on building sea defences for my country."

"Oh, and why's that?"

"'Cos my country's the first to be flooded as sea level rises."

"Well, that's unfortunate… And anything you'd like to say to the world, young man?"

"Yes… All the oil refineries had better watch out…"

There was a slight pause as the presenter squirmed uncomfortably. Things weren't going too well for him. "I see… Um… Presenters shouldn't have to deal with this. Ha ha." He waved Tane away. "Next, please… Now we have Chockice from Tibet in the Himalayas. We're moving to Asia, folks."

Choekyi came tentatively in, looking small and thin, speaking quietly. "I like to build water pipe and pump for monastery, so monks get water for drink and cook."

"Nice one, Chockice...." The presenter heaved a sigh of relief, placing his notes firmly on the table. "And your message for adults?"

"Compassion most powerful force on planet."

"Ah, thank you. Good presenters do bring out the best in people..."

The scruffy hostel cat then suddenly appeared and jumped up on the table, knocking over the presenter's water glass and soaking his notes. The presenter hastily shook his now unreadable notes. "Oh dear! I'm sure we can make it up from here." He gazed hard into the camera. "Cats make a programme look so authentic, don't you think, viewers? As you can see, we're indeed live here today in Hawaii. Who's next?"

Wilga came in tentatively, with her usual bare feet and messy blond hair all over her face, not really wanting to be in the public eye.

"Um... I'm an Aboriginal from Australia. I'll win so I can pay to get my parents out of jail."

"Oh, now there's a good idea!" the presenter laughed. "And I'm sure you've got a good message for us all."

"Yes... Listen to the indigenous peoples who know how to live in balance on the Earth."

"Ah well... Not many left are there, my dear? Oh dear... Next!"

It was Moz's turn. He strode in, cap back to front, eyes blazing. "I'll win so I can feed the people of my home town in Somaliland."

"Is that all?" The presenter asked, looking a bit lost without his notes.

Moz turned on him angrily. "See this here?" He fingered the scar on his face. "Have you ever had to fight for a crust of bread?"

The presenter was taken aback and Mr Dung nearby put a restraining hand on Moz's shoulder.

"Let's move swiftly on. Well, don't children have some interesting ideas, viewers.... Who do we have now?"

Lana entered, looking shyly around at all the cameras. "I'm going to make a movie about the nature fairies in Ireland."

"Well that's very Irish, if I may say so."

"And plants have as much rights as we do to live here."

"Very sweet, thank you, dear.... Any more? Ah, it may be our Russian competitor?"

Victa marched in wearing her black skintight onesie, looking fierce and imposing. The presenter took a step back. "Well?" he said to cover his unease.

"No question I will win," Victa said. "And use money to bribe officials, so no conscription into army, and continue martial arts training to win international gold."

"Of course you will," the presenter said nervously. "And your message to the adults?"

"You will listen carefully... You have messed up our world. Put it back together. Do not mess with kids." Victa then went to give a martial arts demonstration. Her brows furrowed as she focused on channelling life-force. Then, moving mesmerisingly slowly, she suddenly shouted, "Haa!", and went into a lightning high-punch move, which startled the presenter so much he fell over a chair and ended up flat on his back, looking up at the cameras with a pained expression.

Victa looked down at him, showing no emotion. "Winning comes from creating a force so others yield without being hurt."

"Ah yes, indeed..." He pulled himself up from the floor. "I think we can believe our Russian contestant, viewers." He waved her on, dusting himself down. But suddenly aghast, he put his hand to his head. His red nose went white as he mumbled, "Oh no! Where's my hairpiece?" Then he spotted something which looked like a hedgehog in the puddle on the table that the hostel cat had made... Ah... He reached over just as the cat decided hedgehogs should be pounced on...and drew back his hand to smooth over the bald bit of his head, which now looked nice and shiny... And laughed hard, trying to cover his embarrassment.

"Oh dear, yes, well.... Do we have any more? Ah...one more I think."

Kai came in, nervously biting his lip. He had to do this. All the other kids had been brilliant. So he could do it too. "Hello… Um… I promised my granny when she died that I'd look after my mum, so I need to win the race to pay for her to have a big operation, so she can go back to work."

"I see… And would that be useful?"

"Well, yes…she can do the washing-up again."

"Good heavens! Ah, okay. And your message?"

Kai stopped… He hadn't thought about this. "Um…my message is… Please look after all the animals 'cos…'cos…we need them to help us move into the golden era."

"Oh." The presenter was even more surprised at this answer. "And how do you know that, young man?"

"The dolphins told me."

"Ah…okay. How quaint.. Don't kids have wonderful imaginations, viewers?"

At this point the hostel cat decided the presenter's lei looked worth playing with. It was violet-blue, which he particularly liked, and was big with dangly flowers. The cat jumped up onto the camera nearest the presenter and took a flying leap into his arms. Expertly, the presenter stretched his microphone arm out in front of him. It got tied up with the violet-blue lei, but made a lovely platform for the cat to pose on in front of the camera, and to swipe at the dangly flowers.

"Gee, this'll get the ratings up," the presenter whispered, before saying triumphantly to camera, "So you can see, folks – the animal kingdom is on our side."

That was when the cat spotted a large fly that had landed on the presenter's large nose...and took a swipe with his paw, which missed the fly but caught the presenter on the large nose with a sharp claw. The presenter let out a screech and threw the cat off. Unfortunately, onto the cameraman, who yelped and knocked the camera onto zoom – showing superb footage of the painful scratch drawing blood on the large nose, which dripped decoratively onto the once suave and sophisticated white tie.

"Well, that just about wraps it up for today, folks. Make sure you tune in on Wednesday when we'll be filming live from the race itself. Who will win this epic race? Find out then."

The red light went out. They were off the air. The presenter collapsed gratefully onto a chair. "That went well, then. Thanks guys. We'll edit it and show the bits we like for the later viewing, though I'm afraid it's too late to change what's gone out." He stroked the bald bit of his head and sighed. "Could be some interesting headlines tomorrow."

The hostel cat sat nonchalantly grooming himself, long pink tongue easing all the ruffled bits

– all in a normal day's work.

Kai heaved a sigh of relief that it was over. "That was strange, wasn't it?" he said to Lana. "Sort of unreal."

"Yeah, Egghead," she said. "Like play acting… The nature fairies say best to look for real-life drama."

"Like dreams…" said Kai.

29
Heart-lights

"Surprise! Surprise! Flies in pies! This is your favourite supercool dolphin dream guide here."

"Thought you'd got rid of Degbert..."

Splosh! Splat! Kai is soaked by the biggest splash ever. He wipes the waterfall from his face and the sting from his eyes.

"Phinn, that was the best kerploosh…"

"No, I'm seeing how high I can jump and the landing went wrong. Bellyflop!"

"I'll need my suit of armour to try…"

"Good idea, 'cos we're going on a journey today."

Kai groans. "No more scary journeys, Phinn."

"It's okay. It's the Snow Dolphin who's taking us. It's a great honour. You can stay in human form. But best behaviour."

"I'm always on best behaviour, Phinn!"

"Except when your heart-light tells me something different."

Mmm… Must be careful what my thoughts are saying, Kai thinks.

"That's the challenge..."

While they're chatting there's a parting of a flowing silver wave and the beautiful Snow Dolphin shimmers before them. "Thank you, Dream Guide," she beams. "Greetings, Young Human."

Kai nods respectfully.

She kerplooshes.

Immediately Kai feels a shivery whoosh down his back – confirmation of something important happening.

"I would like to show you some human

behaviour," she sends. As usual her words don't come from speaking but through thoughts.

They follow her shining white body, flying across wide open seas to a strange shoreline – a bay enclosed by rocks. Here there's a commotion… Anger. Shouting. Disquiet. Humans have forced dolphins into the bay. To commit a dreadful crime. To kill them. The sea runs red with blood.

Kai can't look at it. He turns away. "Why?"

"Greed!" sends out the Snow Dolphin, sadly. "And no respect for the natural world. See the shadows on the heart-lights of the humans doing the killing."

He feels like he wants to be sick, but whispers, "What can be done about it?"

"When human thoughts become peaceful, then violence on Earth will stop."

Kai tries to work out what this means.

"It's coming," she insists. "The golden era of peace and love is coming, but we have to help bring it in."

There it is again, he thinks. The golden era…

"But look… See the other humans trying to stop the slaughter, in their boats. See their heart-lights all fired up, shining with love for the dolphins."

Kai looks.

"So, understand, it is the thoughts behind actions that matter."

Sweet!

A cloud appears in front of the scene and Kai thinks the Snow Dolphin has gone, but she says, "Young Human, we are grateful for your work as a go-between from dolphin to human. Now humans can hear the information long awaited."

Before Kai can think about this she continues, "We have a gift for you. Come!"

They fly through dream clouds to a familiar shore, to a familiar town, to a familiar house…

They're hovering near the ceiling in Kai's sitting room at home in England.

He gasps.

"They cannot see you or hear you. Just watch."

Mum is in her wheelchair, her head bent forward. He can see a picture in her mind of a research lab. He knows she's yearning to get back to her work but he never knew what she'd been studying before becoming ill. Now he can see a sign that says 'Alternative to Plastics'. Somehow he understands it's for love of him…her son. He can see her heart-light is full of love.

"Love you, Mum," he whispers. She looks up and smiles as though she senses something and says something gently to Dad.

Dad sits opposite and Kai sees he's wearing a work jacket with a logo on the pocket which says 'Bio Poo Bags – so natural you can eat them'.

Looks like there's been some changes at his work. Cool!

Kai can see Dad's heart-light too. His eyes open in surprise, for Dad's heart-light is also full of love. But there's a shell of something hard around it, built by a long-felt sadness, which Kai can see in the picture in Dad's mind. The picture is of Dad as a small child crying inconsolably – inexplicably abandoned by his parents. Kai understands that the hard shell was built so he can't be hurt again.

He watches.

Dad is looking at the TV. There are pictures of the pre-race show, with all the kids and the presenter and the hostel cat. And then it's himself that's being viewed – his words, 'I promised I'd look after my mum.'

Kai can see tears on Dad's face. He can see the shell on his heart-light cracking and love shining through the cracks.

Even in his dream body, Kai can feel his own heart welling up, and a lump in his throat. Through it all he has a happy feeling that his family are connected by love.

As if in confirmation, to his amazement, Dad gets up and starts washing up. What is going on?

And then Kai feels his heart nearly bursting as Bandit bounds into the room. And, even more amazingly, Dad bends down to fondle the dog's ears.

Things are different at home.

Bandit suddenly stops nuzzling Dad and lifts his

head directly to the ceiling. He whines and his tail starts wagging furiously, sending him round in circles.

"Turnin' turtles! Time to go," says Phinn.

The vision is gone.

The Snow Dolphin is gone.

They are back in a familiar Hawaiian sea with brother and sister dolphins playing nearby. Leaping in joy.

There are clicking giggles. Phinn tickles Kai with his flipper.

Kai laughs and grabs the flipper and they dive to a shallow sunny seabed and search for coloured pebbles.

Kai woke, the dream dancing in his mind. He puzzled about Dad. But the memory of Mum was clear. It made him even more determined to win the race for her.

30
Rice Pudding

The sun wasn't yet awake as all the kids followed the Kahuna through the shadowy trees down to the little beach, alongside chirping frogs. Rain was blocking the stars, but there was no need for head torches. Merely the coming of the sun's light gave a tiny glow to shiny wet tropical leaves. Enough to find the way.

"Not seeing much is good," said the Kahuna. "Our native Hawaiian ceremony is about seeing inwardly. And this is cleansing rain."

Kai was happy in the dreamlike state of half asleep anyway, with just the cool sand at his feet, reminding his body to move.

At the ocean, the soulful call of the Kahuna blowing the conch horn sent him into an even more relaxed state. The rain had stopped and the gentle lapping of waves accompanied the dance of white surf catching the first golden rays of dawn.

The Kahuna blew the conch horn again, and chanted and sang. The sound was haunting. Kai felt it stir something deep and ancient in him.

There was the magic of aloha in the air.

Across the bay the mountain waited.

"White Mountain welcomes your run, carrying peace for Mother Earth," the Kahuna said to them all. "Now... Let go of your stresses. Walk into the ocean and become part of it. Immerse yourselves completely and come out renewed."

They began to go in. Victa tore in fast, attacking the sea, determined to be first. Hank smoothly dived into the waves. Tane flowed as though part of the water, listening to the song of the Great Sea Spirit. Moz charged in, splashing wildly. Josee and Wilga helped Bibi, who had taken off her leg and was not that confident in the water. Only Choekyi decided he would prefer to sit on the beach and quietly meditate.

Kai tentatively waded in until the sea was lapping at his chest, before he suddenly stopped. All very well putting his head under water in his dreams, but this was different. He'd really have to do it. He started shaking, not sure he could. Lana had been watching him. Without saying anything she grabbed his hand, and distracted him by pointing at two little turtle heads bobbing alongside, beaks open in a toothless grin.

"Take a breath, now... One two, three."

He held her hand tight. Ducked down. And they were under. And....it was no different from being in a dream. They came up smiling at each other. Then stopped and stared in wonder. Across the bay and the lower lava reaches, over to where the mountain stood, a stunning double rainbow spread across the dawn sky. The conch horn sounded long and deep.

Mother Earth had accepted them.

Just then, with no warning, the sea became alive with dolphins, as though they were part of the rhythmical flow of the waves. They rode in, jumping and flying free. Light underbellies flashing. Beaks smiling with joy. Some blew from blow holes, creating high cascading fountains. Some trilled, whistled and clicked in harmonious song.

They swam in circles around and between the

kids, each one coming up close to Kai and brushing against him, meeting him eye to eye, like a brother. He stood open-mouthed in awe and rapture... Never had he experienced anything so thrilling, so beautiful, so completely filling him with wonder. He knew the salt water on his face was mixed with tears of excitement moved from something deep within him.

Then they started jumping high and spinning with great acrobatic leaps, filling the sky with mastery and boldness.

Everyone was so focused on the amazing display that no one had noticed Bibi. She'd been lying on her back, kicking with her one leg, rising with the swell, but had been tipped over by a wave. Her face was in the water and she couldn't get her body righted. The swell was carrying her out further. She was swallowing water and spluttering, arms flailing in alarm, face momentarily rising to the surface, panicked with fear. Above her was a sense of a dragon-shaped cloud that seemed to reach out to the dolphins.

A small group of dolphins, reacting as one, quickly surrounded her. Touching her with reassuring nods of foreheads and lifting her with beaks, they nudged her over onto her back. Then they held her head and the stump of her leg, giving support, so she was balanced enough for them to push her into shallower water near the beach.

Mr Dung had just arrived. He rushed in to grab her and carried her out, laying her side down on a towel. She coughed up sea water and spluttered for a few minutes and then managed to sit up and say to Mr Dung, "I'm fine! I can do everything myself, you know!"

He smiled at her, relieved. She was none the worse for wear.

The Kahuna came to sit with her and rubbed her back comfortingly. But Bibi pushed her away. She was already back to her usual, spiky self, annoyed at having to be rescued, and barely listening to the old woman saying, "You don't have to have a hard shell around you, you know."

Bibi looked away at the continuing dance in the sea.

"The dolphins can sense when humans are vulnerable," the Kahuna continued. "It's then, when hard shells are gone, that they can be there for people."

Bibi took no notice.

"It's okay to be sick or weak, and let others help you."

Bibi still said nothing, but the Kahuna was satisfied. She knew that a seed of healing had been given by the dolphins. And she knew they'd been called by Bibi's dragon spirit guide.

The show was over. But still the dolphins played in the bay. Waiting for something. The kids stood in the shallows, watching.

Mr Dung was gathering things he'd brought. He stood up and waved a pile of papers. "Look! This is great! These are the peace messages from children all round the world...including friends at your schools. They're pledges for respecting the natural world. I've printed them onto rice paper so they'll biodegrade."

He placed them on a little boat he'd made out of sticks, lined with leaves, and pushed it out to sea, declaring loudly, "May the natural world accept these fervent wishes that humans live in peace with all beings." He pushed it out further, so it was buffeted and spun with each wave. "They'll later be spoken out from the mountain top. But now we ask that the natural world take the essence of the messages to the part of the mountain below the ocean."

The little boat rocked up and down perilously, but stayed afloat.

Kai stood to the side, holding on to rocks in deeper water, watching so intently he almost didn't hear a familiar kerploosh, followed by, "We're here now!" as a dolphin with an unusual nick in his dorsal fin slid by, displaying a cheeky grin.

Kai smiled to himself.

"You're late, Phinn!"

"Turnin' turtles! I wanted to miss the acrobatics! I need a bit more practice as a physical dolphin. These guys are out of my league!"

"You need to take the flips more seriously! See it! Be it!"

"So you do listen to the lessons."

"No, not me."

Phinn came round and shoved him with his forehead from behind.

"Oy. We're not in a dream now… This is my world, you know."

"Quit fooling about then… Listen…the dolphins have a message…"

"What?"

"We will play our part."

"That's it?"

"Yup… They accept responsibility for the peace messages on the lower underwater part of the mountain, so the whole of it will resonate with the young humans' messages."

"Okay…but…"

Phinn wasn't listening. He'd swum over to investigate the little stick boat. By now it was soaked and about to sink.

He went alongside, opened his beak and Kai watched in horror as he proceeded to eat the messages. Swallowing them whole. Every last one of them.

Gulp!

Kai waded over to the little boat.

"Phinn, what are you doing?" he cried.

"Turnin' turtles! Helping of course – carrying the messages to the bottom of the mountain as requested."

"But Phinn... You ate them."

"How else am I supposed to carry them in a physical dolphin body?"

"But...but...dolphins don't eat rice."

Phinn spun round in a tight circle, "How d'you know?"

"Well...dolphins are meant to only eat fish."

"Are you sure?"

"Pretty sure."

"Dumpin' dogfish! What will it do to this dolphin body?" He put a flipper onto his belly area and burped loudly, looking around. The other dolphins were staring at him strangely and easing off back towards the open sea.

Meanwhile the Kahuna was calling everyone together on the shore.

"I've gotta go Phinn," said Kai. "See you later, in dreamtime..."

Phinn seemed rather stunned by the turn of events.

"The Snow Dolphin will know what to do," Kai shouted over his shoulder, heading back to the beach.

"Who're you talking to?" asked Hank.

"Oh...him," said Kai, vaguely waving at the sea... He wants to be part of it all."

Hank looked at him strangely. Tane raised his eyebrows, intrigued. Great Sea Spirit had been singing of peace but the song had changed for some reason. Whatever, it was time to listen to the Kahuna.

"That was a beautiful cleansing ceremony," she said, "but from now until you start running in the early morning, try and hold kind thoughts in your mind. Then you'll have the strength you need." There were looks of disbelief from the kids. Surely this was the time to get psyched up to beat everyone else, to be in the winning frame of mind?

But she continued, "And here – I want to give you each something." She held out tiny green parcels of salt wrapped in shiny leaves from the taro, the local potato-like plant. "Carry them with you in your running backpack, up the mountain. We native Hawaiians believe they will protect you. A hui hou – see you later."

They all went back to the hostel to prepare their kit, eat loads of food and rest.

Hank and Tane headed for the hostel computer. They had an even busier day ahead. They were having fun on social media. It was all because Tane had one day been listening to Great Sea Spirit singing of plentifulness in the sea – "Plenty for every creature's needs, from far-off waves to deep seaweeds" – that he'd suddenly had an idea. It was to set up 'Bid for a Kid', a game for people to place money on the winning kid of the race. Hank had helped him with techie knowhow to make it happen. And since the TV show had been aired across the world, they were getting inundated with cash. "Better not tell Josee – she'll think it's greedy," said Hank and Tane agreed.

"Bibi is the most popular to win at the moment," Tane said, looking at the figures. "With Victa coming a close second."

"The race is getting unbelievable attention by the media," said Hank, excitedly. "We're super-celebrities now."

"Just make sure you get some sleep yourselves," said Mr Dung, checking on them. "Early start tomorrow…to get to the top before dark."

He was passing round a few copies of peace messages to each of them, to carry with them on the race. "So you don't forget the big reason behind this…to draw attention to the Natural World Crisis…and to make a difference…" He gave Kai the messages from his friends at school. "And here, there's a note from your mum and dad, sending love and wishing you luck."

"Thanks, Mr Dung."

Somehow that made Kai really nervous. The

time was getting close and everyone seemed to be striding about looking confident. He went to the hostel dining room and stuffed himself with carbohydrate – pasta and pizza and then more pizza, to give him energy for the next day. And he hydrated himself by drinking as much water as he could, until his body felt overflowing, like the time he'd not turned off the bath taps at home… Then he filled up the water bladder in his little running backpack and went to rest on his bed, thinking, 'somehow I've got to gather strength'. Happily there was no-one else around. He cuddled up with Phinny and soon dozed off.

"We're here now!"

There's big splashing of a dolphin dream body, practising high acrobatics.

"Phinn. I thought you'd be busy sorting the peace messages."

"Turnin' turtles, I'm preparing for that."

"How can acrobatics help?"

"It'll make me better in the physical body."

"Fishbrain! Looks like a dolphin dithering dodge to me."

"It's supercool really."

"So what did the Snow Dolphin say?"

"She said I was in trouble for snatching the peace messages, trying to look important."

"Don't tell me you blamed your ego, Degbert, again?"

"Of course..."

"Fishbrain! He's really messed up this time."

"She said I now have to be responsible for playing the part of the dolphins to spread the essence of the messages around the base of the mountain. This is a forty-five-mile swim away from the island and then down into seriously deep waters, like nearly 6,000 metres."

"But you can't dive that deep."

"I can if I think I can."

"Phinn... Be sensible! It won't be a dream... You've got to do it in the physical dolphin body, so you can only hold your breath for a short time. How long d'you think?"

"Not much more than ten minutes. Dumpin' dogfish! It won't be nearly long enough." He gave a rather pathetic kerploosh.

Kai had never seen him so down.

"I'll find a way. I'm used to thinking anything possible."

"What, like poo on a deep-diving fish?"

"Something like that... Hmm, nice idea... Who's the dream guide here?"

"Have we reversed roles?"

"Not at all... Just testing you... Supercool... I must go... I've gotta find a way. Otherwise I might have my assignment taken away..."

"Yeah. Go and do it, Phinn."

He didn't move.

"What're you waiting for?"

"Kai..."

"Yeah, what's the problem?"

"My physical dolphin body has an awful tummy ache..."

31
Ready, Set, Go!

The next morning, Kai also had a tummy ache. Too much pizza! Should've had vegetables! But good thing he'd stocked up, as he felt too sick with nerves now to eat.

This was it. The race was about to start. The kids were gathering at the beginning of the road they would follow. It was 3am.

The sound of waves sloshing didn't help his tummy. But here he was on the black rocks at the edge of the town bay, bending down to touch his fingers into the ocean. That felt important.

His head-torch cast a little circle of light through the darkness. In one direction to the tumbling tops of surf rolling in. The other towards the impossible top of a mountain over 4,000 metres into the sky.

But no light at his feet. The rocks were wet. His trainers slippery. He fell over.

Thwack!

Like a kerploosh, it stunned him into action mode, but this was in the physical, not a dream.

Rocks not water.

He bashed his thigh heavily.

Dratbag!

It stung cruelly. And the frustration stung his eyes. He could feel the warmth of blood running down his leg, so splashed it with water from a wave filling a dark rock-pool.

The Kahuna spotted him wincing in the light of the head-torches and saw the blood. "Ah, Dolphin Boy!" she said reassuringly, "The elemental beings of the ocean will be happy that you leave a bit of yourself behind."

"Not a good time for it," he grumbled.

"Now is important," she said. "The power time..." She offered him a hand to steady him back off the rocks. "There's been an exchange of energies. The elemental beings will run with you," she said, "endorsing your name, Kai."

He looked at her questioningly.

"It means ocean," she said.

It didn't surprise him. Just at this time, both asleep and awake, it was who he was.

"Ocean brother," said Tane overhearing, "you might like to know that Great Sea Spirit is singing of a lone dolphin just over there in the bay...in a stressed state."

"Thanks, mate," said Kai, while thinking anxiously; go well, Phinn.

Here he was, about to run from sea level to summit on the upper part of the mountain. But more worried by what was going on with Phinn from sea level to ocean floor, on the lower part.

He tried to focus on what was in front of him.

Lana was wallowing in nerves, fiddling with her running backpack.

"Have you got the dream stones, like the nature fairies asked?" she checked.

"In my pocket," he nodded.

"Even the nature fairies living in the trees on the coast here are jumping up and down, saying how important the dream stones are," she said. "It's as though the natural world has an internet which joins up everything across the whole mountain."

Kai smiled, thinking of the Snow Dolphin's insistence that all is interconnected.

"I'll wait for you at the top, Egghead," she grinned.

The other kids were milling around, shouldering each other in the patchy light, like a wound-up spring waiting to uncoil.

Moz was nervously chucking pebbles around.

"Don't do that," spat Josee crossly, trying to change into a t-shirt stating 'I'm the winner' on the front and 'follow me' on the back.

Wilga ignored them, seemingly in shock like a lost zombie, while Victa was strutting around staring people down, in spite of the dark.

Tane was now getting in everyone's way by sitting and repeatedly putting his trainers on and off to get them comfortable. Hank buzzed around searching out the camera teams hiding in the bushes.

Meanwhile Bibi annoyed everyone by twitching up and down on her blade leg, which glinted ominously.

There was tension everywhere.

Only Choekyi was calm.

Kai walked silently beside him as they headed into the town, grateful for his presence. He was different from the other kids. Serene. And, strangely, like he'd already learnt what he, Kai, had still to learn. He found Choekyi's steady energy helped settle him down, easing his tummy ache and painful leg.

Near the library was displayed a huge lava rock. The Stone. The starting point of the race. Here, the headlights of a vehicle cast a ghostly shadow as the runners assembled round it.

Camera teams were poised nearby, but thankfully the big-nosed TV presenter was nowhere to be seen.

"Ironing his tie," said Bibi.

"Discovered he's allergic to cats," said Josee.

Mr Dung looked around at the kids, dressed in shorts and t-shirts, wearing running backpacks, for a run of forty-two miles up a steep mountain at altitude, expected to take sixteen hours. He felt unbelievably proud of them, of the way they took it all in their stride, apart from understandable nerves, as if they did this every day.

He tipped back his cowboy hat and spoke to them quietly, mindful of the sleeping town. "This is a sacred place for the native Hawaiians. Ancient legend says that whoever could lift the Stone would unite the people. And the most noble Hawaiian king, a man reputed to be super-tall, was said to have lifted it when he was a kid your age. Isn't that great?"

Kai pulled himself up to his full height on hearing this, surprised at how it gave him confidence.

"And he did indeed bring the people together in peace," Mr Dung continued. "So it's the perfect place for you to set off to tackle the impossible.

Facing the impossible is where you learn and grow…and find you can do more than you thought."

There were murmurs from the kids, who were keen to get going.

But first the Kahuna held up twigs from a special tree with ten round fruits on, one for each of the runners, and placed it on the Stone. "This will hold the loving essence of the Stone, giving you wisdom and courage for the duration of the race. The physical merely reflects the essence."

Sounds useful, thought Kai, thinking of Phinn spreading the essence of the peace messages.

"Okay guys," said Mr Dung.

They all lined up in front of the Stone.

"Good luck to y'all."

Ten white lights shone from torches on the front of ten heads. Ten flashing red ones on the back.

"It's up to you now… A long way…so take things steady. But make sure you drink at least every twenty minutes. And have a decent rest at the Visitors Centre… Thirty minutes is ideal to work with the altitude. That's as far as the vehicles can support you. After that it's the trails. I shall be back and forth in the jeep. And the Kahuna has kindly agreed to be in the ice-cream truck."

The kids all cheered. And the media crews took this as a cue to close in on the runners. Among them…oh no!…the big-nosed presenter, complete with dashing flashing Micky-Mouse tie, and braces to match, holding up particularly smart white trousers, with his microphone in hand.

"This is news, folks!" he shouted. "How exciting! You cannot miss this. An international first, here in the Hawaiian Islands! An ice-cream truck as a support vehicle on such a unique and important race. What a scoop!"

The slime-green ice-cream truck proudly stood there ready. On the sides was written 'White Mountain delights' with tantalising yummy pictures of cones with various coloured toppings painted all over it. The speciality being 'volcanic explosion with chocolate and orange rocks'. On the back was, 'Pay attention to the children'.

"See here, viewers! This is its supreme moment. The owner will get great advertising exposure on the morning news and be able to sell the company for a million dollars! Who wants to buy an ice-cream truck?"

The sleeping town was now an awake town.

Mr Dung thought it time to get the show on the road. He faced the kids. "Everyone okay? Right! Be the best that you can be!"

Kai had heard that before somewhere...

"And never stop believing you can do this... You're each already a winner to me..."

I can do this, thought Kai, taking a deep breath. All the effort, all the training, all the heartache has been for this.

"Ready... Set..." The ice-cream truck played an inspiring jingle, almost drowning out the big-nosed presenter shouting, "Who's going to win, folks?"

A starting-gun firing would have been perfect, but it was a loud shout...

"Go!!!!"

Kai let the others rush off and began running gently, mindful that his muscles were spiky at having to work so early in the morning, watching the flashing red lights of Bibi bounding off with Victa not far behind, the others following. That was his first mistake. He wished he'd stayed close on this first bit. It was very dark. Scary on his own. There were only isolated street lights, which were dim to prevent light pollution at the summit observatories.

He looked up at the billions of stars above. They made him feel small and insignificant, but filled him with a feeling that this challenge was for something much bigger than himself, so really worthwhile.

In no time at all the fuss and noise was left behind.

His muscles settled and he fell into an easy jog. It meant he could spend time in his thoughts... Though he didn't really want the ones that came – mostly anxious ones about Phinn.

Being a dream guide, Phinn'd be okay, even though he wasn't entirely sure how that worked. Except he did know that if Phinn messed up and couldn't sort the peace messages properly, then his dream-guide assignment would be terminated. That would mean no more contact. That was very worrying.

Kai's thoughts jogged with him through the town, steadily uphill, following the flashing red lights until all the houses were passed, and he ran on the verge of the road, into complete darkness.

What was even more worrying was, knowing Phinn, his Degbert would try and be a hero without calling in help. He would maybe try and use his physical dolphin body to carry the essence of the messages beyond what it was capable of – down into the real scary depths. Down to where it was dark and cold and there was huge pressure. And not being that experienced in the physical dolphin body...what then?

Phinn! Phinn! pleaded Kai in his mind. Please, just for once, be sensible...

He saw a red light just ahead and sped up, so that he could perhaps chat and take his mind off his worries.

It was Wilga. He ran up alongside. She was going at an-easy-to-chat pace. "How ya doing?"

"Hiya... Okay, thanks. The mimis have shown me a picture of a tortoise, so I know I have to run at my own pace and not worry about keeping up. Then I can run forever."

"Like in the hare and the tortoise story...slow and steady wins the race?"

"Too right," she smiled.

"It must be a big incentive to know that to win would get your parents out of jail?"

"It's everything to me. Lawyers cost a fortune. The only thing they've done wrong really is be native aboriginal. Okay, they were drunk and caused big trouble. But it all comes from the history of our land being stolen and our culture squashed by invaders, who live in a different way from us. Same as indigenous peoples all round the world.

"The native Hawaiians too."

"Too right... Here on the lava fields, where there's a magical energy, the mimis, being little rock spirits, are sending pictures of the sadness of the land yearning for the old balanced ways. Reminds me I must win..."

Kai didn't know what to say. He understood Wilga's dreams, but he desperately wanted to help his family too. He didn't want to think about Dad – it was complicated. But he imagined Mum after a successful operation, walking about with no wheelchair and happily doing her research on alternatives to plastics. He knew he was going to give everything he had to try and achieve that.

He took sips of water from the tube of his pack and started running like a hare, leaving Wilga behind.

He had no idea if he would be able to keep up the pace.

32
Stupid

The night seemed endless. The uphill relentless. On and on into the blackness. Just the white line at the side of the road to follow with his little light. Where was everyone else? How come they'd gone so fast? Already it seemed like he'd been running forever, yet it was early on in the race. He didn't want to look at his watch. It'd merely show the impossible task ahead.

This place was out of time altogether. His legs were doing the moving, and he was just flowing with them. Just him and the blackness, as though he was the blackness itself, but also a big sort of nothing that was everything as well.

The thigh he'd fallen on was throbbing, but he didn't want to stop to look. It was too scary, as he'd have to face the loneliness and the intensity of just him and nothing. Then he became aware of the stars far above and felt like he was a spaceman running through space... Lost...but also at home... Where was the moon? Why no moon? At least that would be a friend... He just needed a friend.

Suddenly there was the noise of a vehicle chugging and headlights lit him from behind, throwing his shadow, giant-like, before him. A slime-green friend drew up alongside. Window down and a voice shouting, "Well done, Dolphin Boy! Stopping just up ahead. You can grab what you need..." And it was gone into the night.

Ah!

The next bit was much easier as he knew he was about to come up to the ice-cream truck. By the time he saw the headlights parked he could once again see a handful of red lights the other side. And one runner at the open window of the truck, ice cream in hand. It was Josee.

"Recommend the 'slime lime'," she shouted as she rushed off.

"I'm with you," shouted Kai, quickly grabbing the two offerings the Kahuna held out, so he could run alongside Josee. He found he had a banana in one hand and a cone of deep blue with something sticking out of it in the other.

"Looks like you've got 'dolphin dream'," she said.

"How come?"

"Jelly babies in it...shaped like fish... Dolphins love jellyfish ice cream."

Kai smiled.

He gobbled the banana and tackled the cone. "Yum! Good to run and eat ice cream at the same time."

Josee laughed in delight. "Yeah, I'll enjoy all the different flavours before catching people."

"Want to try 'dolphin dream'," said Kai, passing over his cone.

She took it and was about to lick but then handed it back. "It doesn't smell right, Kai," she said, screwing up her nose. "Must be connecting up with your dolphin friend. Feels like he's in difficulties."

Kai didn't say anything, but felt a pain grab him in the heart. He threw the ice cream into the bushes, hoping the birds would like it, and sighed heavily.

Josee chatted on. “I’m going to chew my Columbian coca leaves. They’ll give me super energy as well as help with the altitude. I’m determined to win and help my village stand on its own feet, growing its own crops. I can do it, you know.”

“I wouldn’t doubt it,” said Kai absentmindedly, with his thoughts on Phinn.

Josee talked about living in the Amazon rainforest as they ran, and Kai found it helped the time pass. By the time the ice-cream truck had passed them and resettled, he could just see a faint light stirring in the east.

He’d made it through to dawn.

They must have been running for three hours. It was a good feeling. His body felt as though it always ran, designed for this natural rhythm.

At the truck he drank water, so he wouldn’t have to refill his water bladder, grabbed a couple of cereal bars and kept going. Josee waited for a ‘mango fandango’.

It was a grey drizzly dawn. Suddenly he could see, though like in a cloud. He thought it would make things easier, but the misty forest reminded him there was still most of the mountain to climb. The timelessness of the dark had gone.

He sped up by lengthening his stride, finding that concentrating on breathing steadily helped his energy. Every ten breaths he allowed himself to look around, until the forest thinned out – a good sign of being higher. So, coming into the next stop, he treated himself to a 'ginger ninja', along with water and a banana.

"You're doing great, Dolphin Boy," said the Kahuna, "but a bit of bad news... Josee told me about her smelling dolphin difficulties with the 'dolphin dream' ice cream. And Wilga said that explained the picture she got of a dolphin caught up in abandoned fishing nets. It must be the one who ate the peace messages. I'm afraid it doesn't look good."

Kai looked at her horrified, blinking hard. "What can we do?" he pleaded.

The Kahuna shook her head, but then her face brightened, "I have an idea who might be able to help. Want a rest in the truck?"

He shook his head and rushed on.

"Pace yourself... The others aren't that far ahead," she shouted.

That gave Kai a boost to try and put his worries to the back of his mind and he kept his stride until at the brow of the next hill he spotted two red lights ahead. Coming closer he recognised the figures of Tane and Moz. Tane seemed to be struggling, running like a baboon on a hamster wheel.

"What's up?" said Kai, drawing alongside and seeing Tane's pained expression.

"Sore feet," he said. "The burns from Long

Mountain…"

"Rest in the truck," suggested Kai.

"Yeah, I'll have to. And plaster them up."

"That'll help," said Kai. He knew Tane'd stop at nothing to prevent his country from disappearing below the waves.

It wasn't long before a jingling truck chugged by. They waved it down and Tane collapsed into the front seat. The Kahuna would soon sort him out.

Kai and Moz grabbed water. Then looked at each other sideways. Neither said a word. Both knew this was the moment they were up against each other – the time to show who was stronger.

They set off at a faster pace. Never mind about saving energy for later. There was only one thing that mattered. Breaking the other one.

The road ahead was long and straight. The cloud was lifting. They could see a couple of red lights and the forest opening out to lighter scrub in the distance. Before long they'd be in the dark brown of the old lava fields.

They ran alongside each other on the hard shoulder of the road, not concerned about speeding cars. Better than the bumpy verge. When one inched ahead, the other one caught up. Neither was going to be beaten.

Moz was fuelled by long-held anger at his harsh, tough childhood, having to fight against starvation. He resented Kai's softness. And Kai, present worries buried, was fuelled by built-up anger at being unfairly bullied, since that first day on the plane. Now they were able to express it.

They ran faster and faster. Neck and neck.

A runner's red light came up. It was Lana. They tore past without saying a word. She shouted after them, "What're you doing?! That's stupid!"

Still they ran at breakneck speed. Strong young bodies trained up to race.

But the anger was running its course. The point came when it was spent. They both were tiring. Moz turned and gave a shove to send Kai into the bushes. Kai anticipating it, grabbed the strap of Moz's backpack. They both tumbled arms and legs all over into the spiky vegetation and rolled to a stop in a heap.

Neither had won.

Chests heaving, panting hard, they glared at each other.

"Your farts smell," said Moz.

Then an extraordinary thing happened. They both laughed.

After a few moments, Moz got up, dusted himself down and, shaking his head, started jogging on. Kai wasn't sure he had the energy to get up. His muscles were trembling. He was dripping with sweat. And he felt guilty. Had he jeopardised his chances of winning the race by running a personal battle? What would Phinn say about his behaviour? For sure, he'd blame his ego. And now Phinn was caught up in fishing nets anyway…

Lana came plodding up, steady and calm, not looking like she'd been running for six hours.

"I know," he said. "It was stupid."

She offered him a hand and yanked him up and he staggered with her to the next vehicle stop, which was the jeep. Mr Dung insisted he change his clothes, drink serious amounts of water, fill his water bladder and take time to sit and eat cereal.

While he was eating, Mr Dung updated him on the race. "Victa's ahead at the moment, but Bibi's closing in fast. And Hank's doing a good steady job at keeping them in sight. But it's still anybody's to win."

Kai listened but was more concerned about not being alone. By the time he was ready, Lana had gone on. He felt sad. Guess she's got a nature fairy movie to make, he thought miserably.

"You've got this," said Mr Dung, gently shaking him by the shoulders to encourage him.

Kai nodded, eyes down, too tired to speak.

"Keep an eye out for nene geese. There's been sightings up the road. According to the Kahuna, the nene is an important guardian spirit of the land."

Kai started moving, thinking: don't see how the nene can help me. Don't know how I'm going to find the energy. No strength. So how can I keep going? No idea. All alone. Feel lost. What am I doing? This doesn't make sense. It's hopeless. I'm no good, just like all those years of feeling unloved by Dad. And knowing I'm useless 'cos of being different from other kids. Tall with a funny-shaped head. And scared of swimming...

His thoughts were all rambling and jumbled. And he was utterly annoyed at himself for being stupid and squandering all that energy.

Left leg, right leg... Left leg, right leg... His feet dragged. His heart wasn't in it. What's the point? he thought. I can't do this.

He jogged on past the twenty-mile marker. Well, at least I'm nearly halfway, he thought. But it didn't help.

As if in confirmation, the sun came out and it began to get hot. This – illogically – made him feel crosser. Thankfully Mr Dung had insisted he wear a cap. But the heat took its toll. He was exhausted. He stopped running and started walking. Then, annoyed at himself again, he looked around, checking if anyone had seen, and returned to jogging. Slowly. Then slower still. His body seemed to have forgotten how to run. His legs felt heavy, so very heavy. It was as though his mind had no more energy to drive them. There was no reason to keep going.

I've had it, he said to himself.

I can't do this.

I'm giving up.

He collapsed down on the grass verge, dragged himself to a big lava rock to lean against.

And waited to be picked up.

33
Magic of the Lava Fields

Kai felt peaceful about giving up. He'd given it his best shot. Cool… He could now go home.

He relaxed against the rock and shut his eyes, his hand idly picking up some lava gravel. It felt alive! Weird! As alive as he was! He opened his eyes to see. Just dark brown crunchy stuff that had poured out of the volcano at some point…

Earth blood… But it was talking to him!

Wooh!

Strangely, he felt sure it was the nene – guardian spirit of the land – who was doing her job and showing him the aliveness of the natural world connected up all around him. He shook his head. He was seriously tired. That sprint with Moz had taken it out of him. He was in that drained, vulnerable state when his mind had no barriers to thoughts that didn't make sense.

He tried to think sensibly; what's the lava giving off? Energy waves of some sort… And if his body was giving off waves at the same vibration then his thoughts must be in tune with it, surely? That would explain why he felt as if it was talking to him.

So what? Now he could go home.

But the talking went on: 'going home to tell your friends that you gave up. Is that an option?

'Going home to tell your dog, after all that time apart, that you couldn't even finish it. You were tired.

'And to tell your classmates at school, after the teachers trusted you to come back and tell everyone about it, when you were carrying their messages – the promises they, and others around the country, had made to help the world. But it wasn't so important.

'And the media at home. Yes, you and Lana

representing all the kids in Europe. But you couldn't be bothered to finish the race.

'And what about Lana, waiting for you at the summit, when you have to say sorry, couldn't manage it.'

Failure!!! The word stung to the depth of his being. He'd have to carry it all his life.

He looked around at the lava landscape – desert blacks and browns, with spiky bushes and beige grasses. Survivors of tough conditions. They didn't give up.

He threw the lava gravel down in disgust, dragged his body up, and started running again.

He didn't feel alone any more.

Once again his legs were somehow managing to jog gently, while the rest of him sat enjoying the ride. "Thank you," he said. He had no idea who he was talking to.. Maybe the swathes of lava... Or the nene goose... Or the mountain itself... They were one and the same. As he was one and the same with them. Whatever... He knew he had help, so was grateful and went with it. He was in that timeless space. And, as if to confirm it, the cloud came heavily down all around him and he ran through a bright mist.

Thoughts drifted: 'what about my supercool

dream guide, with his physical dolphin body caught in a net?... Will he survive? Has he lost his assignment? Will we ever speak again, through my soft cuddly Phinny, my gift from Granny?... Hmm... And remember when she was dying... I promised her I'd look after Mum... A promise not to be broken... I have to get myself together and somehow win this race... That's the most important reason to keep going... I will keep going... I can do this...'

Then he saw in his mind a picture of Granny saying, "Kai dear, Phinny was given to me by my grandmother – your great, great grandmother – who loved dolphins and believed they carry important information for people." He almost stopped as it hit him. Of course... That's what I could never remember. That would explain why Phinny was old and battered. So now it's doubly important to listen to Phinn... But is Phinn okay?

There was a cry from behind that startled him, and Tane appeared.

"Feet good now," he said as he bounded by. It certainly looked like it.

I must be running slowly, thought Kai. He'd been in his own world. But at least he was running and he'd settled down again into a rhythm that worked for him. As far as he knew he was now ahead of two of the other kids; well, that's only seven more to pass...

The ice-cream truck was waiting at the road junction at mile twenty-eight. He grabbed food and water and was about to keep going when a shout stopped him.

"Dolphin Boy! Here!" It was the Kahuna, standing by a pile of rocks on a little mound. He walked over, muscles stiffly easing at the strange and unnatural motion.

"This is the Hill of Standing Feathers," she said. "Come and join me. I'm honouring our native Hawaiian ancestors." She gave him a potato-like root, indicating for him to place it on the flat top of the pile of rocks. "This is taro, which is the staple food of the Hawaiians. We mix it up, like mashed potato, and everyone eats from the same dish, known as poi. The rule is...with poi on the table, no one can speak ill of anyone."

Kai nodded, sure of the importance of accepting the customs of the land. And knowing that the lava-fields magic was all tied up with it. Somehow the boundaries between things here weren't as defined as elsewhere.

"Hold the ancestors of the land with love in your heart-light and they run with you," the Kahuna confirmed. "Now...I must tell you. I spoke with Bibi about your dolphin caught in the fishing nets. I asked her to see if her dragons could help."

Kai looked at her astounded; surely someone as spiky as Bibi would never want to help?

"Remember poi," said the Kahuna. "Now, go!"

He gave the message to his legs to start running again. There was a delayed response. Then they obeyed. His body felt heavy, but his heart felt lighter.

It was a relief to turn onto the narrow, twisting White Mountain road. Now only six miles and 800 metres in height up to the Visitors Centre. Looking back the way he'd come, he could see Wilga and Josee deep in conversation not far behind. It spurred him on to find the energy he needed. The first bit was not steep. It was still misty ahead, so he couldn't see far, but he knew from their acclimatisation trip to the Visitors Centre that the road suddenly became diabolically steep. He felt quite anxious about it, but plodded steadily on, passing a sign that stated 'Altitude Sickness Can be Fatal', reminding him how he'd found running at altitude much harder than walking. His anxiety levels went higher.

But all Mr Dung's training advice, so boring at the time, had not been in vain. He'd suggested preparing for difficult bits by calming the mind, repeating positive phrases, over and over.

So he tried, "I'm strong," which helped his determination. Then, "I'm supercool," which made him giggle and think of Phinn too much. So he changed to, "This is to help my mum," which was too complicated. Finally he reverted to what he sometimes used at school, "I can do this!" And purposefully strove on with every step.

He was just rounding a sharp bend reciting his phrase when he stopped dead. He'd almost bumped into a little family. There was a beautiful adult bird with round body and long creamy neck, topped with a black face. Beside her were two fluffy beige chicks.

"Hello nene," he said. It had to be her, though thankfully normal goose-size.

She eyeballed him with a knowing look, completely unafraid.

She'd come to confirm her presence and show him her babies – hope for the future.

Just at that moment there was a roar. Kai turned to see a car tearing by, gathering speed for the ascent. When he turned back, the geese had gone. Disappeared into thin air. He blinked and ran on. This time his words were, "I'm natural world," and he continued, not fighting the ground but flowing with the lava at his side and the wind at his back.

After a while the ice-cream truck chugged by, Kahuna waving. She must have waited for Wilga and Josee, who would now be past the junction and not far behind.

Then came a car with windows down and cameras pointing at him. He ignored it. But there was shouting from the next one, harder to ignore. The big-nosed presenter was leaning out, microphone in hand, "And here, folks, we have our European representative, who speaks with dolphins. Can he catch up Africa and Asia? That's a tall order! But then this is the tallest mountain. What d'you think, viewers?"

The voice trailed off as the vehicle turned a sharp corner and came to a standstill at the bottom of the diabolically steep bit. The vehicle in front had stopped behind the ice-cream truck that was struggling to move. The camera crew were out trying to push it.

The big-nosed presenter jumped out, indicating for a camera to keep filming. "Well, this shows us how steep the road is, folks. The ice-cream truck's in trouble. The slope's like a black ski run and we're having to push our granny up it in a wheelchair!"

The truck's tyres screeched and there was the smell of burning rubber. It almost moved. The crew rocked it up and down to help. A bucket of ice cream fell out of the side display window and rolled under the wheel just as the tyres got a grip and squashed the bucket.

Squelch!

A volcano of speciality 'volcanic explosion' exploded out of it.

Splat!

It just happened to be where the big-nosed presenter was standing so he could be filmed centre-shot in the action. So it just happened that it completely plastered his Mickey Mouse tie and his face above it. Only a large nose could be seen. Then there was a tongue…and a hand holding a microphone, wiping eyes, which made it drop all over the smart and sophisticated braces.

A slightly croaky voice said, "Well, it's important to try the ice cream, folks, and er…I can report that this is the best I've ever tasted."

Having got the ice-cream truck going, nobody wanted to stop, so the presenter was dragged into the vehicle by his braces, spreading speciality 'volcanic explosion' all over his seat and his smartly pressed not-so-white trousers. And the vehicle sped off.

Kai heaved a sigh of relief at the resulting peace and quiet. Then put his head down so he couldn't see the steep road, shortened his stride and settled into the challenge of the climb. It wasn't long before he was puffing hard. Not only was this the steepest ever, but the altitude was kicking in too. He tried thinking of something else. Inevitably it was Phinn. He thought of their fun journeys. Then remembered Phinn reciting, "See it. Be it!"

Of course! Visualise! He imagined himself arriving at the Visitors Centre with everyone else there. He saw the buildings, the white stone dolphin, even the Ranger. He pictured it all. Yes! He could do this. It brought positive feelings.

More cars sped by with shouting, but he was too busy concentrating to take any notice: hold the focus. I can do this! See it. Be it! When he eventually did look up he saw he was almost up the diabolically steep bit. There was a big rock beside the road at the top. Taking a gulp of water, he pictured the rock coming down to meet him.

He tried the same technique up to each hairpin bend. Slowly, slowly his legs ate up the miles.

At last, he saw the Visitors Centre through drifting mist, just as he had imagined it. And a glimpse beyond towards the cinder cones, with... could it be? An impossible tiny patch of white... Snow? He felt a tingle down his back.

Panting hard, he arrived. Where was the Ranger? Kai irrationally wanted him to be where he'd met him before. Instead he spotted a sign to a room in the information building for the racers to rest, feed and hydrate for their half hour. He staggered in, feet heavy like concrete, legs like jelly, lungs gasping and collapsed onto a sofa in relief.

That's the easy thirty-four miles done. Only eight miles to go... But 1,400 metres of height to gain... And much less oxygen up here. He could feel his eyes wanting to cry. He pushed his face into a cushion to stop them. No way – not in front of everyone.

He looked up to check that they were all there. Josee and Wilga followed him in and also fell in exhausted sprawls onto the sofas, breathing heavily. Victa was prowling in front of the food table, shoving in potatoes and guava jam, then headed for the door to set off, scowling heavily as though trying to cover up a big internal battle. Even so, he saw that she stopped at the white stone dolphin to send life-force energy.

Hank was filling his water bladder, obliviously spilling water over the floor. Bibi was spreading grease on the stump of her leg and cursing. Tane was re-plastering feet. Moz was stretching muscles. Lana was in a complete daze. Only Choekyi looked at ease. How does he do it? wondered Kai.

His own body was completely done in, like it would never move again. He had no energy left... No idea how he was ever going to keep going...

He felt himself become heavier and heavier, all the way from his feet through to the top of his head. His muscles were seizing up. His brain giving up. Eyes closed tight shut, he began drifting into sleep.

He was shown a dream picture. It was of a

dolphin with a nick in his dorsal fin. There was a sense of carrying something precious. The dolphin was receiving a mighty boost of life-force energy, like a bolt of lightning, and heading full-speed away from the surface of the ocean, downwards into the cold depths.

34
Against the World

Kai heard a loud splash.

Kerploosh!

And he felt a whoosh down his back.

He drifted further.

But there it was again.

Kerploosh!

He felt a bigger whoosh… A call to action!

Wake up, Young Human!!

He felt enveloped in a loving heart-light. And saw in his mind the mesmerising eyes of the Snow Dolphin. Shining! Behind her, there was a pod of brother and sister dolphins, leaping and diving, travelling mile after mile across wild seas. Putting up with plastic dumped in their home. Coping with noise from ships. Trying to avoid being killed. But still journeying onwards. Keeping on keeping on...

Kerploosh!

Action!

Kai opened his eyes and dragged himself up to standing, trying to focus, shaking his head. The monster oxygen-sucking slime blob was now inside it banging with a hammer. He managed to stagger over to the food table, feeling too nauseous to eat, but thinking of Mr Dung's advice, "Look after your body. Eat before you're hungry. Drink before you're thirsty."

He gulped down vast amounts of lemon water. Filled up his water bladder. Then forced himself to swallow a bowl of yoghurt with fruit salad. It stayed down. Then remembered, "Salt for muscle cramps." So he gobbled a few handfuls of salted peanuts, and pocketed some. He felt sick and had a tummy ache, but it would hopefully be enough fuel for the next six hours to the top.

So far so good.

He hobbled outside and stood stretching his legs

in turn to try and loosen the muscles. The road he'd come up was still shrouded in mist, clearing around the Visitors Centre. There were tourists about, having lunch and enjoying this wild and beautiful spot with glimpses of far ocean views.

He spotted the Kahuna placing what looked like sugar cane on a framework made of sticks behind a little gate and felt the happy connection with the ancestors of the land.

But then he was distracted by the conversation of a tourist couple seated on a bench nearby. He heard the word 'dolphin', so moved in closer to eavesdrop.

"I just heard a dolphin was rescued today," the man was saying. "He was caught up in old fishing nets. Lucky to survive apparently. The nets were tied to driftwood which kept the dolphin above water so he could breathe."

"Who rescued him?" asked the lady.

"Fishermen. They cut him away with their knives. Evidently they'd been heading to fishing grounds elsewhere but were drawn to the area where the stricken dolphin was by a dragon-shaped cloud. Strange! Apparently they thought they'd better investigate as their boat was called, 'Sea Dragon'!"

Kai didn't want to hear any more. It seemed Phinn had survived one disaster only to head straight off into another. His heart was pounding.

He took a deep breath.

He thought of Phinn, always wanting to be the hero, saying, "I was hoping for something more warrior-like..."

But then he remembered him, in dream-guide mode, saying, "Pay attention to the song singing inside you." Yes...he, Kai, could hear that heart-song. It was clear as a bright sun on a sparkling sea. It was to keep his promise to Granny and win the race to help Mum get better.

He would pay attention.

Never mind the rest time-out. It was time to get running.

He kicked his bum with his heels a few times to ease his stiff legs into moving and turned uphill.

There was a familiar jingle as he passed the car park and spotted the big-nosed presenter standing by the ice-cream truck, microphone in hand, speaking to camera and a group of fascinated tourists. He was looking dishevelled and clutching an obviously nauseous tummy, having failed to take into account that he might suffer from altitude.

Someone handed him a 'cute dragon-fruit' cone which he licked as he spoke, trying to look normal. "Mm...this 'cute dragon-fruit' certainly is...dragon-like..." He leaned back, trying to give his tummy more room, catching his braces on the 'yummy choices' sign.

"So folks, who will win this exciting race? My money's on South Africa, first in before the break... But wait... The pack's coming out now..." He listened in to an earpiece. "Good Heavens! There's been a surprising development. You won't believe who's shot ahead..."

He tried to step forward to ease the cramping in his tummy, "Gee whiz! Doesn't altitude make everything an effort..." He pulled harder. Then suddenly...

Twang!

The braces released and hit him hard on the back.

Whack!

His head went rapidly forward so his big nose went straight into the ice-cream cone. Lifting his head to the sky, nose a cone-shaped horn, like a rampant rhino, he wrenched it off, saying, "Yes folks, definitely the best ice cream ever." The cameraman quickly zoomed in, as the sound had been lost due to the presenter speaking into the ice-cream cone instead of the microphone, but smoothly changing hands, knowing an ice-cream cone doesn't have the same acoustic properties as a microphone. "Oh folks, you must all come and try some..."

And viewers across the world watched as the big-nosed presenter vomited into the microphone.

Kai could still hear, "And we have authentic

sound effects here at altitude, folks..." as he left the clapping tourists behind. He wondered what the presenter's heart-song could possibly be... And why the ice cream was reminding him about dragons...

He jogged up a little further, to where a group of journalists and camera crew hovered. Mr Dung stood in front of them, waggling his fire-ravaged cowboy hat by the start of the trail to direct the runners. "Well done, Kai... You're doing great! Keep drinking water. There's two supply points if needed. See you at the top."

Kai paused, making an aloha hand sign, "For your son."

Mr Dung smiled sadly, but returned the gesture saying, "For the world." And encouraged him with. "Go! Go!... Choekyi is currently ahead after the break. There's been jostling, but Victa's leading the group of Hank, Moz, Tane and Lana, all close together. Then Wilga. But they're not far in front of you."

Not far in front, but Kai knew every one of them, even Lana, was against him... A lonely feeling that he was against the world...

He took a deep breath, taking in all the oxygen he could – happily this also seemed to take in a feeling of being part of the natural world all around – and started off.

Running gently, he followed the dusty rocky

trail west around the mountain, thankfully not too steep. There were a few tall dry flower-heads bending back and forth in the harsh wind and he wondered if Lana's nature fairies enjoyed this high home. Apart from that it was a lunar landscape of desert gravel – grey, rust and brown – tasting gritty on his tongue. He looked down on a sea of cloud, feeling cold in spite of coming out into the sun.

As his muscles eased he lengthened his stride until he came to a sharp bend north. He looked up at a terrifyingly steep scree slope – a slope of loose stones, tumbling and clattering at the attack of the kids scrambling to climb it. Lana was leading, stepping lightly up in her large sun hat, tightly tied against the wind. She was closely followed by Moz, sturdy with his back-to-front cap. Hank, Victa and Tane were panned out, not far behind, finding their own route. They were all stopping every few minutes to catch their breath. Wilga was just starting up. Choekyi was nowhere to be seen.

A scuffling noise behind made him look back as Josee joined him, puffing hard. "Wooh! this looks like fun," she gasped, taking a handful of leaves from her pocket to chew, first smelling them with approval, as though bringing the energy of the Amazon rainforest to help her in this mountain desert land.

Just behind her, Bibi, in bright yellow kit, was rushing up, looking annoyed. She pushed past them both and took her own way up the scree slope. This was difficult terrain for her false leg. It was hard enough to gain grip with trainers on, but her blade slid awkwardly at every step. She tackled it furiously, cursing loudly and calling on help from unseen dragon friends.

Kai was in the thick of it.

The race was on!

He decided to find his own route and be steady. He'd learnt the importance of trying to keep thoughts peaceful – not wasting energy fighting himself. So, he took a big breath. Then, visualising himself at the top of the scree slope, thanked the mountain and set off, scrambling upwards. Though still feeling he'd forgotten something important…

He soon found that going straight up involved two steps up and sliding frustratingly one back down. So he tried short zigzags. This was better. It felt natural. His body had trained bounding up sand dunes! It suited his long legs and he found himself powering steadily up at a pace he could breathe without gasping or having to stop.

He barely looked up as he passed Wilga, who was determinedly pushing back her wild hair and chanting to herself in between wheezing. But there was no mistaking passing Bibi, cursing as she struggled. He almost felt sorry for her, knowing how much winning and building a safe house meant to her. But it felt brilliant overtaking her, and gave him a surge of energy to tackle the others, spread out before him.

Victa shouted angrily at Kai as he, slowly but surely, scrambled by. Then went back to noisily yelling, "Haa!" at each step like a battle cry, with a focused, determined look that might itself kill an opponent. She panted hard between each step. The altitude's getting to her, thought Kai. Nothing else would've slowed her down, knowing that winning meant she could give up even the army that she was besotted with to continue her overriding passion of life-force training... Tough – but she was certainly tough!

Tane was grunting like an upset bear as Kai passed him. His face was contorted in pain from troubled feet.

Next Kai came up alongside the expensive trainers of Hank, and wondered why he even needed prize money... Kai was about to power past when he realised that, in between gasps, Hank was mumbling in his gruff great grandfather voice, "Aloha, boy..." Gasp. "Dolphin..." Gasp. "Nick in fin..." Gasp. "Peace messages..." Gasp. "In deep trouble..."

Kai gulped in surprise and looked across at Hank's face, which seemed to be oblivious to what it was saying. Hank had lost it. He was in another world. This was the time of the ancestors.

"Great Grandfather, we honour you," said Kai, trying to keep level and hoping this was what the Kahuna would say.

Hank's face remained the same, contorted in effort and pain, but the voice continued, "Too deep..." Gasp. "Cold..." Gasp. "Pressure..." Gasp. "Can't breathe..."

Kai felt frantic and helpless and desperate. "But Great Grandfather, what can we do?"

The words that Kai dreaded the most came back: "Too late." Gasp. "Lost consciousness." Gasp. "Body sinking."

"Noo!" cried Kai.

"Pack of dogfish coming to clean up body." Gasp. "Dogfish coming..."

35
Ocean Deep, Mountain High

Moz was waving at Kai to come nearer.

The steep scree slope was thankfully easing as he scrambled up alongside and glanced into Moz' face. It seemed he'd coped with their sprint. But Kai could see that he was done in – sweating hard, scar livid purple and a haunted empty look on his face as though he'd given everything he had.

"The yellow-bellied..." gasped Moz.

"What d'you mean?" panted Kai.

"They've got the peace message essence."

"How d'you know?"

"The yellow-bellieds deep in the ocean have been linking with me. I'm getting a huge bed of writhing sea snakes underneath a dolphin..."

"How does the dolphin look?" interrupted Kai.

"I can't see. I can only sense..." Moz stopped to grab his breath. "I just know the dolphin released the essence and the snakes are now carrying it."

"Poo," said Kai.

"What?" said Moz, puzzled.

"The dolphin would've pooed the essence onto the snakes."

"Oh..." Moz still looked confused.

Kai could see the others gaining ground behind. Time to speed up. "Cheers, mate." He put his hand lightly on Moz' shoulder with, "Hang in there," and jogged on.

The trail now became a gravelly winding snake to follow between bigger rocks and stones and old black lava. He was able to run rhythmically again. His mind gave the order but the body had other ideas. Nothing happened. Eventually it responded grudgingly. One leg and then the other... Kai felt as though the body wasn't in charge. His mind was hovering above and directing with, “C’mon body! We can do this.”

He was still feeling disjointed as he approached a supply stop with drink and food laid out on a large rock and a sub-ranger speaking into a walkie-talkie. “Choekyi’s passed. Kai’s about to and Lana’s here.” She was sitting with a shoe off beside a beautiful dry plant that looked like a cluster of silver swords.

He knew he couldn’t stop, as the others behind would also be running harder after the scree slope, and catching up. Grabbing a drink, he shouted, “Okay?”

“Blisters!” she shouted back. “Egghead, wait… The nature fairies here are telling me you must hold the dream-stones at the lake.”

He waved and kept on running, trying to concentrate on his feet and on the rugged land ahead, steep but doable. It crossed a kaleidoscope of black, gold and brown lava stones, with a few brave grasses. He stuck to the gravel trail now, sometimes heavy sand, but clearly marked ahead, winding between high red cinder cones.

Step after step after step…

The sun shone brightly in between fast-moving cloud, but it was beginning to get cold. Should’ve grabbed more clothes to wear, Kai thought… Well, there’s one more supply stop, somewhere. A little higher up he could see north-facing pockets of white on a couple of the cinder cones. Mid-summer snow! Even with climate change! This was the domain of the Snow Dolphin! His jumpy mind started drifting into a dream-like state... wondering what would happen to her when the snow completely disappeared. Kerploosh! He was awake again. And the shock almost brought him to a standstill.

I mustn't stop, he thought, now that I'm in the lead... And he felt a burst of pride... No...that's wrong... Choekyi's out there somewhere... I've got to go faster to try and catch him. He lifted his head to search the trail ahead with his eyes. Untrustworthy, tired eyes. For it was then that he saw something extraordinary. Along the dark skyline, silhouetted against bright clouds, he saw a boy in a maroon-coloured jacket running... Though not exactly running. Kai shook his head and blinked... The figure was bouncing along, long hair flowing behind...with more like the motion of a bird than a human...barely touching the ground with his feet...and unbelievably...with lightning speed. It didn't make sense at all.

The cinder cones soon covered his view of the higher trail. And he forgot what he thought he'd just seen as his focus harshly returned to his complaining legs. Muscles were burning and felt like lead. "C'mon legs. Do as you're told," he told them... And suddenly giggled, realising... Wow! I sound like Dad!

Dad. Just the name made him tense up. As it had all his life. But then he remembered his strange dream journey with the dolphins and seeing Dad's loving heart-light underneath the cracking hard shell. Was there a chance for a new relationship? Could he make things happy with Dad, now that he understood the hurt-shell had made him like he was? To be abandoned as a child must have been devastating. Maybe Dad would talk to him about it one day…or maybe it didn't matter anyway. He resolved that in the future he'd work to be friends.

But what was it that had brought about changes in Dad? Could it have been him, his son, going away? Strange as it seemed, could he even have missed him? Whatever, Kai had the strong feeling that when he went home things were going to be better. This thought gave him a sudden boost of energy and even more determination to win the race.

The race… He looked behind him, but wished he hadn't…

There were three figures there, and more further back. Bibi was almost upon him. In the next second she bounded by, blade glinting in the sunlight, shooting up stones behind, a triumphant look on her face.

Barely had his mind processed what had happened when there was a determined cry and

Victa passed too, yelling words that sounded as though they were bolstering Russian troops for battle.

This made him speed up. But his legs complained too much, so he slowed back to his steady pace... Again he could hear the crunch of running steps right behind him. Josee was tailing him. He tried again to speed up. This time it was his lungs that complained. He couldn't get his breath... No! c'mon lungs! He still couldn't breathe properly. His body stopped and doubled over coughing, which caused the monster slime blob in his head to bang even more. His body hadn't even asked him!

C'mon!

Josee shot past saying, "I'm the winner!"

He stood upright. The cold wind was biting and whipping up dust into his face, creeping into his eyes. He turned away and took a huge breath of dust-free air, muttering, "Thank you, White Mountain. I'm natural world."

The figure of Hank was in sight, gaining ground behind him. He badly wanted to see if Great Grandfather was still around but didn't dare loiter.

He started running again at his steady pace and soon came back into a rhythm. Left leg, right leg... Left leg, right leg... He pictured Mum standing tall in her workplace. A sign behind her saying 'Biodegradable Alternatives to Plastics. No more Human Damage to our Planet. This is the New Era.' It lifted him with a fierce joy, whether for Mum standing up or for the difference her research would make, he didn't know. It was all tied-up, one and the same in this important reason to keep going. More important than anything he'd ever done in his life before.

"I can do this..."

The steepness increased but he managed to hold the rhythm. Left leg, right leg... Left leg, right leg... He knew his body was cold, but separated himself from that thought. He knew his body was exhausted but separated himself from that thought too.

The trail came round a cinder cone. He saw Josee sitting on the side, one leg in the air, rolling from side to side screaming. "What?" he shouted. "Cramp!" she screamed back. He looked behind to gauge how far back Hank was. Delved into his pocket and shoved a handful of salted peanuts into her hand. Then rushed on, barely having broken his rhythm.

By the time he could see the next supply stop, with another sub-ranger on a walkie talkie, he was shivering from the cold. It didn't look far to go but seemed to take forever. Time stood still. He was running, running, running and still it wouldn't come nearer. Something was getting scrambled here. He could hear the gravel crunching at his feet. And feel the wind attacking his arms, pushing left arm, right arm, left arm, right arm , but he was losing something, not quite attached to himself… and the mountain seemed to be spinning. What's going on? "Cmon," he muttered. Why am I so dizzy?

At this point Hank pushed past, but Kai couldn't seem to get his thoughts in order to say anything until almost too late. Then merely a desperate cry of "Great Grandfather!"

Hank turned and stared with a vacant look. The wind was blowing back into Kai's face. It carried words he could just make out, "Aloha boy... Strong dolphins..." Words of hope. But that was followed by "Bad...bends..." and then he couldn't hear any more.

Oh no!

He knew divers got 'the bends' – fatal bubbles of nitrogen in the blood from rising to the surface too fast. His brain couldn't compute any more. Again he cried from the depth of his being, "Phinn!"

He couldn't think… Could barely feel… Hardly knew if he was deep in an ocean or high on a mountain. Neither places for bodies to survive.

As he stumbled up to the supply stop – a few bags in the dirt – he mumbled, "Cold," and with a superhuman effort managed not to collapse to the ground, legs shifting from one to the other. Too scared to sit. Never get going again… He was handed a fleece top, but struggled to put it on as his hands were too numb to work… The sub-ranger helped and zipped it up for him, and then the process was repeated with a windproof jacket. Water somehow found its way to his lips. If I linger, he thought, I've had it. Keep moving, whatever.

"Your position is fifth. Choekyi's first, then Bibi, Victa and Hank," the sub-ranger's words drifted towards him as his legs took him onwards.

He barely registered the bent-up figure of Hank at the side of the trail being sick. He wanted to stop. But his body didn't.

As the trail snuck behind a cinder cone out of the wind he finally felt some feeling come back to his hands. He began to warm up, and the dizziness lessened.

Phew!

A sign came up, confirming he was now at 4,000 metres above sea-level. That meant only 200 metres more in height to gain – getting nearer. But off to the side, close by, was a surprise for his eyes. He tried to take it in. Nestled between the cones, a side track led down to a beautiful little green lake.

Wow!

It was a strange colour. A sort of shimmering metallic emerald, sharp against the browns of the desert rocks and the deep blue of the sky.

He remembered the Ranger had said scientists couldn't work out why the water doesn't drain away through these porous rocks. Physically, it shouldn't be there. Was it a sacred doorway into the natural world? An oasis of magic. There was a tiny patch of white snow nestling on the far side. Kai felt a tingling whoosh in his spine.

He halted and stared in wonder at the lake. Sensing a strange and clear feeling from it. Then he spotted a figure bending down on a rock at the edge of the water in a maroon windproof jacket. One hand in the water. There was a glint of light coming from his fingers. It was Choekyi, dipping the crystal. He was honouring the Ranger's request to bring peaceful strength for the runners and the children of the world.

Kai watched him, trying to understand the almost bird-like leaping he'd thought he'd seen earlier, when another amazing thing happened. Nobody would believe this either. But he saw it, trickster mind or not. This time, clearly Hawaiian magic. An unseen hand drew a sign across the lake. It was as though an artist had taken a brush and carefully created a masterpiece. Kai stared. The sign was the old Hawaiian symbol of a fish-hook.

It connected him to the ocean. He was hooked...

It was a sign from the natural world. He felt

its harmony and strength. And finally his mind calmed.

The dream stones! He nearly forgot. Delving into his pocket he pulled them out, gently stroking them – rounded, solid and real. As he did so, yet another extraordinary thing happened. Whatever… Go with the natural magic. He shrugged. Looking down on the lake he saw the fishhook melt away. As the water rippled with Choekyi dipping the crystal, Kai watched as though he were viewing a movie on the surface of the water.

The colour of the water changed to blue – a deep ocean blue, with a sense of being a great distance beneath sunlit waves. The faint light showed a fathomless rocky ridge smothered with clusters of red algae. Nearby was a writhing mass of sea-snakes, bodies flattened at the sides for speed with yellow paddles as tails, wriggling in all directions. And dotted on their backs were sparkling lights like confetti. As Kai watched he saw the sparkles being wriggled off and becoming little paths of light, heading downwards into the depths like shooting stars.

Kai smiled as he realised the sparkles were the essence of the peace messages… Little blobs of love sent from children's hearts. And they were heading down to be caught by a waiting group. It was the green turtles. There were three of them.

They paddled around collecting all the sparkles piling up on their shells until they looked as though they'd just been shaken in a snow globe. Shining brightly, they then descended into the cold deep, following an inner magnetic compass. It seemed to Kai they were directing a postman process, giving sparkles of the essence out to various fish to carry on their scales, with instructions to pass it on downwards.

"Thank you Honu," whispered Kai.

There were multitudes of fish on their deliveries, some even swallowing their post, down and further down, until it was almost completely dark. They were way beyond where any sensible plant would want to hang out, except there was light – the light of the essence of the messages. It cast a shiny glow on those skittering to and fro and then diving downwards into the pressure-loaded depths, where special bodily adaptations were necessary to cope with the conditions. He was excited to spot a huge octopus taking part. The octopus swished back and forth, using his jet propulsion, and then went off, returning with a few coconut shells, into which the fish, with some trepidation, deposited and regurgitated all the essence.

Kai marvelled. Coconuts would never seem the same again. The containers were then carried in strong arms with useful suction cups down

down down until the octopus met a swarming army of sea slugs, known as sea angels, with little transparent wings. There seemed to be some sort of conferring going on, during which some of the sea slugs may have been eaten by the octopus, but Kai wasn't entirely sure. Then the essence was transferred to their outstretched wings and they set off downwards, shining like a galaxy of stars.

Suddenly the transmission stopped. The lake was green again. Choekyi was lifting the crystal out of the water. The movie had lasted merely a second of time. But Kai was mystified. Why hadn't the essence reached the sea floor, the base of the mountain?

Whatever had happened to Phinn, at least his efforts, however diabolical or fatal, had not been in vain. This thought gave Kai a great boost. Now it was time for him to play his part too. After all, he was carrying some of the essence of the peace messages, in his backpack.

He put the dream-stones back in his pocket… and gritted his teeth…

Onwards!

Gravel crunching behind made him glance back. Coming up the trail he could see Wilga. Wow! The tortoise steadily approaching. Still wheezing. He couldn't quite make out who was coming behind her. And didn't wait to find out. "C'mon legs. We can do this." He turned uphill and ran, following the trail a little way past the lake. Then it turned between cinder cones up a rise and led before long out onto the road to the observatories.

Getting close.

Only a mile to go.

To the west, the round domes of the telescopes came into view, like far-seeing crocodile eyes peering out of murkiness to watch unknown wonders. Hungry for knowledge.

Kai's feet felt harsh on the paved road. He thought it would be an easier surface, but the pounding reverberated through his body and somehow broke his connection with the mountain. The trail became the road for two long sharp bends, thankfully empty of vehicles. They were now climbing steeply into the sky. The mountain dropped sheer away to the right, over raw volcanic desert and a sea of clouds.

But the road wasn't empty. He could see Victa a little way up the road, just before the first bend. She was jogging and then stopping to gasp for breath every few metres.

We're the same age, he thought. We both go to school with other thirteen-year-olds. She's having to stop to breathe. I'm not. There's no rocks on this bit to throw me. There's no reason I can't overtake her. I can do this. His legs responded with longer strides in spite of the steep incline.

It reminded him about the pledges from children

all round the world. This brought thoughts of his friends at school... They seemed so far away now....but somehow carrying their messages was good...almost as though they were with him...and he was running for them...and children everywhere on the planet.... They all wanted the same thing – to have a bright future. For everyone to be happy and live in harmony together with the natural world, returned to beauty and wonder.

Steadily Victa came nearer. Then nearer still. By the second bend he was almost upon her. He managed to take the inside. She looked up and growled, which forced her to pause and grab deep breaths as he passed.

Hold the rhythm. Left leg, right leg... Left leg, right leg, he told himself... Keep steady. He didn't feel triumph. There was just an empty chasm where his feelings were meant to be. But in a few minutes he knew he had her. He was in front of her.

Yeah!

Only Bibi ahead.

His body was running on some sort of energy coursing through him. He had no idea what or how. It drove him onwards...impossibly...wonderfully.

Left leg, right leg... Left leg, right leg...

At the final road curve he lifted his head up to see the observatories over to the west. There were many, run by countries from around the world. High-tech telescopes searching the heavens, at this the clearest place on Earth. They looked so huge and imposing that he fleetingly understood the desecration of modern science over ancient wisdom. But in a flash that had gone, as an exciting vision came into view to the east. A vision he'd been waiting a long long time to see.

It was the final sacred summit – a deep rust red. Razor-sharp in the evening sun that was beginning to turn the sky pink along with a few high, watching clouds… Zigzag path steep… Possible… Inviting… So close… He could almost reach out and touch it…as he could almost reach out and touch his dream of being there first… At the pinnacle in the sky.

Behind him he could hear the yells and grunts of Victa's frustrations at finding the breath she needed. It sounded like she was catching up. He didn't have to look to know that the others were close on her heels.

And ahead, after the little dip that led off from the road, he could see a figure in yellow at the base of the summit zigzag path.

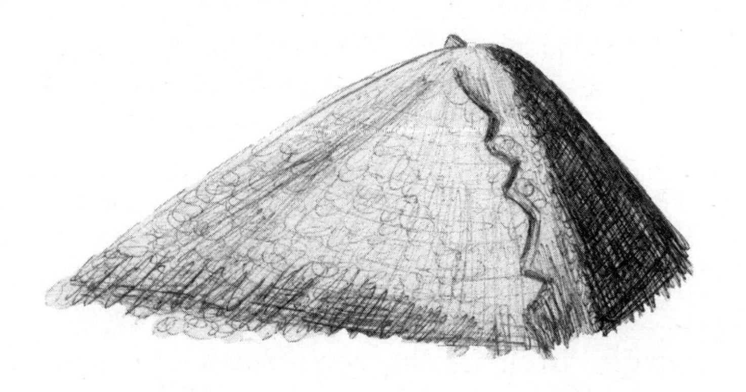

36
Stand Tall Like a Mountain

Over to the west alongside the observatories, camera lights flashed as the world's press jostled to get photos from afar. Thank goodness that was the closest they were allowed. This last bit, up to the ancient burial grounds, was too sacred for photos. But Kai had no energy to think of them…

This last bit was the summit. That was all he had in his mind…and Mum… The difference he was going to make to her life.

He ran the little dip down, revelling in the sense of freedom the short downhill gave him. Legs running by themselves. Like jelly, but running. Then a jolt. It was uphill again. But he couldn't find the energy for it. His legs had nothing left.

"I'm natural world…" he chanted. Then unexpectedly remembered the Snow Dolphin's words: 'Work together with love for the good of everything.' Ah! He'd forgotten the 'love' bit. Immediately he felt his love for White Mountain. And easily imagined love from his heart-light completely surrounding it.

He was not surprised when the mountain's magic worked. The energy was there for him.

In no time at all he'd reached the figure in yellow. On the ground.

Kai looked down at Bibi gasping in pain. The stump of her leg swollen and raw. The socket sleeve where the blade joined covered in blood. She was holding her head in her hands and moaning. Then she tipped her head back so she could see the summit, so tantalisingly close but just so much pain away. Searingly frustrated, she screamed. "I've had it! I can't move!"

He knelt to put a hand on her shoulder. She

pushed it away angrily, shouting, "Go! You go, Kai. Go on! The prize is yours. You deserve it."

He stood and looked up.

The short zigzag path. Empty. Waiting for him.

The summit so close..

Mum…walking…going to work with a big smile.

And Dad, respecting him.

So close…only a few minutes away.

Within touching distance.

All the hard work and anguish fulfilled.

His friends at home congratulating him.

The school honouring him…kids looking up to him with awe…

It's all there.

Just one more superhuman effort.

He can do this.

At last…

He turns…

And looks back. All the other kids are coming off the road onto the trail.

But strangely… Instead of seeing the other kids he sees their dreams… Lana's movie, Choekyi's monastery, Josee's village, Tane's sea defences, Wilga's parents, Victa's martial arts, Moz feeding his town, Bibi's house… even Hank's electric car. And he feels excited about helping everyone's dream…

But what would they say?

How weird. It doesn't make sense.

He hears Phinn's words from…oh so long ago… 'When things don't make sense, listen to your heart… Listen to the heart-song singing inside.'

Could it be that his heart-song has changed?

He turns.

And looks up at his beloved White Mountain, which has helped him get through the race.

A lone tear somehow finds its way out of an eye and creeps down a cheekbone…

Don't wait Kai, he hears in his mind. There are only seconds…

Go on…

Go…

Another picture comes into his mind's eye. A shining white being. The Snow Dolphin. Jumping high. Kerplooshing. Giving him whooshes. Sending waves of light out, engulfing everything, spreading far and wide across the planet.

He feels it in his heart. Like a waterfall of liquid gold. Strength. Certainty. Self-assurance. Love. It swallows up the fear of what the other kids might say.

He holds the love in his heart and extends his heart-light to them all.

At that moment Choekyi floated up, somehow looking calm and fresh.

"Give me a hand, mate," Kai said, bending to pick up Bibi. She tried to stop him, muttering, "idiot!" but had no strength to resist. Choekyi grabbed the other side under her arm with no questioning in his eyes, just understanding. Kai was amazed that the Tibetan seemed to have no interest in actually winning the race.

Kai looked at him searchingly, "How d'you do it, Choekyi? How d'you run fast like a bird, and for so long with so little effort?"

Choekyi smiled and shrugged as though it wasn't important. "Old Tibetan practice of fast feet. Know from last lifetime with long training in cave. Is for higher path. So run with pure mind. Become one with mountain."

Kai nodded thoughtfully. Just for a moment able relate to that.

But no time to think about it.

Lana came up panting hard. "What's happening, Egghead?" she asked.

"Why are we stopped?" said Josee, stumbling drunkenly alongside, chewing hard.

Wilga came next, still wheezing, collapsing onto her knees.

The others, pushing hard, were close behind.

"What's going on?" gasped Hank, looking pale and lost. "There's the last bit to do. The race isn't over. We're not sticking to the rules..."

Kai looked at them. Then pulled himself up to his full height, knowing that for the first time in his life he was standing tall. "We're all going up together." He spoke firmly with a confidence he'd never experienced before, as if it wasn't him talking... "All of us. In a line. We're doing this together... We're all going to win."

"All take higher path," agreed Choekyi, putting a gentle hand on the shoulder of Victa, who was trying to force her way through, stopping her dead in her tracks.

"Like a team paddling a canoe," said Tane, bewildered but sure.

There were looks of confusion, but everyone was so exhausted there was no way anyone could hide their real feelings. And it was relief and joy that was there. There was indeed the feeling of being a team... Stronger together... Invincible together.

Kai raised a fist into the air... "Stronger, faster, higher...together," and they all repeated, "Stronger, faster, higher...together," and joined hands in a common high-five.

It was at this moment that the Ranger appeared. No one was quite sure from where. Kai stared in amazement. He didn't look like the Ranger any more. But the flowing silver hair and startling tattoo on his face confirmed it. He wore black robes with bright yellow and red edges. And leis of waxy leaves which glinted in the evening light. He carried a stick, which he lifted up and drove down forcefully onto the mountain trail, chanting, "Ho'oponopono..."

His deep quiet eyes briefly held Kai's with recognition before he spoke. "This is the place of concord, the place of peace, where everyone stands tall like a mountain. Your actions honour us."

He glanced over at the modern observatories, representing the techno world. Then turned to face the old sacred summit of his ancestors. "You are the seeds for the golden era of the future... Working together with love in your hearts. We thank you."

Choekyi reached into his running backpack and pulled out a long white silk scarf, which was used for sacred ceremony in Tibet, and presented it to the Ranger with a small bow. The Ranger took it and indicated for each person to hold on, so they were all connected.

"Now we are ohana – meaning family," he said and paused, "So no one gets left behind or forgotten."

Kai, mesmerised by the Ranger, watched in surprise as a slow tear slid down the old cheek and flew off to join the wind before it could water the desert ground. "All nations..." he murmured.

There were mutterings of agreement.

"Now," continued the Ranger. "Think of yourselves as an empty cup – so that you can climb up and be filled with your vision for what is needed for the world as you rise up into the future."

"How...?" began Victa.

"It's the magic of the mountain," the Ranger replied. "Believe! The spirit of the ancients walks with us."

Hank too was frowning, trying to work out what was happening, but nodded with everyone else, seemingly stunned by the turn of events. Too exhausted to question. Eventually even Victa let go of her fight and a hint of a smile appeared.

Wilga pushed off her dusty trainers. "Bare feet gives most respect for White Mountain," she said.

They began to move, dragging themselves up the steep wide slope. Kai and Choekyi supporting Bibi limping between them. Moz supporting Kai on the other side saying, "Well done, mate," with deep friendship in his tired eyes. Then the others spread out, holding onto each others' arms on either side so that they were a long line. The ones in the middle waiting for the ones on the end who scrambled to keep up, but at the same time holding up those in the middle. The ones who could move dragging the ones who couldn't. They would do this together. They would.

Slowly...painfully...together... They crept up the zigzag path, up the final slope as the setting sun painted everything with a red glow – the children, the mountain, the ocean of clouds, the sky...

Until in a line, they finally...finally...were at the mount where Mother Earth meets Father Sky – that which connects the land to the heavens. They encircled the pile of stones with its wooden framework where offerings are made, representing the old altar there...and collapsed to the ground at this most sacred of places. Josee and Wilga with arms around Bibi, who, for the first time in months allowed herself to cry.

"May your visions be far-seeing from this place of far-seeing," said the Ranger, looking down on the ocean of cloud which stretched in every direction to the horizon, marking the curvature of the Earth.

He chanted, "Ho'oponopono..." Then placed the stick on the altar as his offering, saying, "May this be a sign that there is harmony...between the new and the old, across the world...as seen by the telescopes of modern science over there...and the holding of the spirit of ancient Hawaii here. They are, after all, both about catching the light..."

And Choekyi placed the crystal beside it – the magic symbol of peace for all the children of the world. It glinted pink in the last rays of the long day. A day no one would ever forget.

Lana joined Kai in placing the dream-stones connecting the natural elementals all across the mountain, both above and below the ocean. And as they read the peace messages from children around the world, Kai felt a fierce certainty surge through him – that the essence of the messages was at that moment spread successfully around the base of the mountain deep on the ocean floor. He smiled to himself.

Supercool!

Mr Dung and the Kahuna had left the jeep at the observatories and followed them up, bringing duvet jackets, woolly hats and flasks of hot chocolate, and joined in with the speaking of the messages.

The bright red ball of fire known as the Earth's sun became orange, then for a brief magic moment touched everything with a warm golden light, like fields of angels, and finally disappeared below the horizon. The sky became alive with stars…more stars than black space between.

That's when Kai knew, he just knew… It was the sea stars that held the essence of the messages on the ocean floor. The sea angels had given it to the sea stars.

And the summit where they gathered glowed in confirmation with an ethereal glow.

Mr Dung stood and stretched his arms out

wide, saying with a wavering voice, "This is great! So fitting... Up here among the stars where you all belong. I couldn't be prouder of each and every one of you... I knew thirteen-year-olds could achieve impossible things. Your story will inspire people for generations to come, to work together for our common future and spread hope around the world."

He paused as a shooting star sped across the night sky, leaving a trail of light in its wake.

Then continued, "You will each now receive a tenth share of the prize money for the projects that you have wished for."

There was a collective sigh of approval from ten utterly exhausted children.

And he went on, "As for myself...I feel my son's life has finally been honoured. And for this I deeply thank you."

No one had the energy to reply.

The Kahuna nudged Kai. "Look, Dolphin Boy... See that really bright star over there. That's the dolphin star."

Kai nodded, knowing in his heart who had guided him to this moment.

37
The Tale Below

The boy cuddled up in bed with his soft-toy dolphin, knowing that it had been a day well lived.

He didn't remember much of the journey back. As with the other kids, he had been happy to be helped down to the jeep at the observatories and driven in a daze, down down down to the hostel, where the air was thick and sweet and warm.

There, encouraged to eat soup… Thankfully no shower – just the wonderfulness of sleep.

"We're here now. Be ready for more adventure!" says a bright, fun-loving voice.

There's a calm turquoise-blue sea…

Boy and dolphin greet each other, rolling over and over in a wave of complete joy, surrounded by sparkling bubbles. They come up for air and spy-hop, beaming in delight.

"Phinn! I was worried about you."

"Turnin' turtles! That's an absurd turd."

"Why?"

"I'm your dream guide. Humans don't worry about dream guides."

"I do. I love you Phinn."

"Love you too, absurd turd human boy."

"Who're you calling absurd turd?" Kai tries to shove Phinn onto his back, but the dolphin, as always is too quick for him and darts underneath the boy and propels him high into the air, to bellyflop down.

Schwash!

Kai comes up laughing and spluttering and wipes the salt water from his eyes. "C'mon then, Phinn. You have to tell me. What happened on your adventure in the physical body?"

"Well..." Phinn wafts his flippers back and forth to stay still – so much easier in a dream body. "For starters, the Snow Dolphin wasn't happy that I nearly killed the physical dolphin body. She said that didn't show respect."

"Nearly killed him twice, Fishbrain. Not clever."

"Well, I gave up counting... Anyway, the body's not in too bad shape, but the tail will never be the same again."

"Oh, why not?"

"Dumpin' dogfish! It has teeth marks. Not pretty...but to me it shows the scars of a warrior..."

"So he'll find kerplooshing difficult?"

"Yes, but he'll stay with the pod now. They'll look after him... But, I might not get another physical dolphin body."

"You are high risk…"

"Turnin' turtles! It wasn't me that put those old fishing nets in my way."

"You were going too fast, I bet."

"I had to practise speed in that body..."

"Then you went too deep…"

"I was researching how far down I could go..."

"And I suppose your ego, Degbert, had nothing to do with it…"

"Someone has to be a pioneer and advance

evolution..."

"You're already doing that by inhabiting a soft-toy body."

"Yup, that's supercool..."

"But you can still be my dolphin dream guide, right?"

"Well, the Snow Dolphin said I can keep my assignment if I see what I discovered from it all... Think she's hoping that my behaviour will change."

"Not much chance of that..."

Phinn swipes him playfully with a flipper... "Dumpin' dogfish, the important thing was the essence of the peace messages did eventually reach the mountain base on the ocean floor."

"How much d'you remember?"

Phinn swims slowly up and down in his perfect dolphin dream body. Eventually he speaks.

"Well... The memory is painful... It was on the drop off of a deep ridge. The pressure was oracle diabolical... It felt as though I was being squeezed like...a..."

"Bucket of ice cream under the wheel of a truck?" suggests Kai.

"Exactly," says Phinn, smiling. "Well, it was pretty much dark...and really cold...and I'd already lost consciousness on one side of the brain... And the other side was so confused it didn't know what was going on."

"Bit like higher up the mountain…" says Kai.

"I s'pose… Anyway, my sonar sensed there was a pack of dogfish coming to eat my body. And I couldn't move. And I suddenly got really scared…"

"Oh!"

"That's when I decided to poo…"

"You really did poo out the essence of the peace messages?!"

"Yup…"

"Phinn! That was really important!"

"I know…"

"Phinn, I can see your heart-light…"

"Okay, it was a happy accident. Anyway, after that I completely lost consciousness."

"So how were you rescued?"

"I was roused by kerplooshing from the pod of dolphins swimming around me. They told me they'd been asked by the Snow Dolphin to stand by and rescue me as soon as I needed help. So, they'd sent a few of their strongest males to dive down, chase off the dogfish who'd started to eat my tail, and nudge my body back to the surface."

"You don't remember that?"

"No. A good thing, though. Unusually for a dolphin, my body got the bends, so I nearly died."

"Again!"

"Turnin' turtles! You're a fine one to talk!"

"Go on…"

"If you'll let me finish… So, the dolphins had to pause bringing up my body. And one went to the surface to breathe in a lungful and came down and blew air into my blowhole for me."

"Upside-down, from his blowhole?"

"Yup."

"Wow! Dolphins are so amazing…"

"We are, aren't we?" Phinn smiles and gives a giggling whistle.

Kai finally manages to give the dolphin a shove underwater while he is off-guard. "So when they eventually got you to the surface and you came to and could breathe again, did they tell you about the peace message essence?"

Phinn splutters, "Yes, the dolphins made sure it went down okay. They said they'd asked the sea snakes to gather it and give it to the turtles, who passed it on to the fish and the octopus and then the sea slugs…"

"They're the sea angels, right?"

"Yup. They like going deep in the dark cold down there… Anyway, at the right moment, they passed it onto the sea stars who crawl about on the bottom and send out messages far and wide to each other around the base of the mountain."

"So all the sea creatures worked together to make it happen."

"Yup..." Phinn looks sheepish. "I had wanted to do it all by myself. Degbert wanted me to be the hero. But, thanks to the love of the dolphins, I became part of something bigger and stronger – more whole."

He stops swimming and nods his beak up and down, looking strangely contented. "I actually felt better being part of a team, working with everyone for the good of everything."

Kai's smile is as wide as the ocean, as deep as the sky... "Phinn, it was the same on the top part of the mountain – all the kids worked together to make it happen."

"That's supercool!"

"And I also learnt that you feel better when you work with everyone for the good of everything. That's so cool... We both had the same discovery."

There's a familiar flash of blazing light and the beautiful white Snow Dolphin appears before them.

"Dolphin Dream Guide, you have experienced your discovery fully. And because of your love connection with your human you both discovered it simultaneously. This is an advanced technique that few dream guides achieve. Well done! You may continue your assignment."

Phinn beams.

"But," the Snow Dolphin says, "You would do well to keep that naughty ego Degbert under control."

Phinn is busy practising a back-dive and not really listening any more.

The Snow Dolphin turns her all-knowing eyes to Kai. "Young Human, we chose you out of all the kids in the whole world. Your adventure has been an initiation – a great test – and you have passed with flying colours. Now we invite you to speak dolphin wisdom for us. The time to share begins."

Kai knows it's important to remember these words. But what is it he must do?

38
The Golden Dream

It was time to consider the dreams of the physical world.

It turned out that while the kids were on the mountain, 'Bid For A Kid' had gone viral. People were intrigued by the race and what thirteen-year-olds were attempting, wanting to support them and do something to help the Natural

World Crisis. And 'Bid For A Kid' presented an opportunity for them to play their part. They just had to name the winning kid and send some money. So when the race concluded without a winner there was a lot of money that couldn't be paid out to anyone.

The morning after the race Hank and Tane considered the problem. This was an amount of money with so many noughts on the end, it was gobsmacking! Was it legal? What to do with it? Hank phoned his father, a top lawyer, who carefully went through 'Bid For A Kid' with his legal team. Yes, surprisingly, it seemed the money was theirs to do what they wanted with. Mostly because no one had ever put money on kids running up the world's tallest mountain before, so there were no laws to stop it!

They called a meeting at the hostel with Mr Dung and the other kids. It was clear that everyone had been transformed by the experience of the race. They each, now, had an intense desire to work together to help the world. And felt invincible. Whoopee! So everyone had expanded their wishes.

Kai knew that everyone's heart-song had changed because of the magic of the mountain.

It was decided that, after giving out the prize money, plus a donation to native Hawaiian education as a thank you to Hawaii, Mr Dung would set up a trust fund with the proceeds of 'Bid For A Kid' for everyone's expanded wishes. This would provide ongoing funds and cover any extras needed on the first wishes. Finally it was agreed they would meet up once a year to support each other and their projects.

Everything was sorted easily, with everyone winning.

"Nations communicating with each other for the good of all," said Mr Dung happily, handing out the mobile phones which Security had hidden.

Kai texted his mum, 'Please arrange operation,' followed by lines of smileys.

Mr Dung continued, "Now, we do need to tell the world about our plans, so let's invite the big-nosed presenter back for a TV show. I feel it's important." Everyone groaned, "Boring!" but agreed when he added, "Let's make it a celebration party in the garden here."

Kai was happy that it involved food. Since sleeping for twelve hours, all his body now wanted to do was eat.

So it was arranged for late that afternoon when the weather looked dry and sunny.

The big-nosed presenter had been waiting for this opportunity. It would advance his career no end. He was delighted that it was to take place outside this time. Fewer cat disturbances!

The hostel staff worked hard and created a long

table of wonderful multi-coloured Hawaiian food in front of a luscious tropical plant backdrop in the garden – the perfect setting for the interviews. And the centrepiece was a gorgeous metre-high chocolate fountain, designed to look like an erupting volcano, with all manner of tempting fruits and cookies waiting to be dipped in the chocolate lava.

Yummy!

The kids were really excited, and couldn't wait for the interviews to be over so they could begin the feast. Definitely worth running up the mountain for! All the agony and exhaustion was already being put to the back of their minds as they recovered. Mostly hobbling from blisters and walking strangely from overdone muscles. But all dressed in the team FNZ t-shirt, with an air of purpose to life.

They lined up in front of the chocolate fountain for photos. The Kahuna came and presented everyone, even Moz, with a lei of golden-coloured flowers, saying, "Hawaii honours you... May you carry the spirit of aloha out into the world."

It was now time for the big-nosed presenter to take it away.

He checked the camera crew were in position, the microphones set and the sun shining so the lighting was just right. Then looked at himself in the mirror with satisfaction. He'd gone for a smart straw hat today to cover his lack of hair. And just a handsome Hawaiian shirt, topped off with lashings of his favourite after-shave to feel debonair and stylish for his adoring public. Unfortunately he didn't know it was also the favourite after-shave of the local population of mosquitos.

"Let's roll, guys! Remember to look at the red light." Then he put on his orangutan-being-tickled face.

"Five, four, three, two, one... Action!"

"Good evening folks in the US and around the world. Welcome to the conclusion of the contest to run up the world's tallest mountain! Here, live in Hawaii. The story of kids from across the planet who've tackled the impossible to highlight the Natural World Crisis." He paused to push away a small insect member of that world.

"Typical of youngsters, they decided to do it their way. They all reached the summit at the same time so that everyone won. Who would've known! Many of you put money on 'Bid For a Kid'...which you've lost... Bad luck, I say! So this evening each kid is going to tell us what they plan to do with their considerable sum. I present to you our billionaires of the future!"

He waved to the kids.

"And starting us off we've got Hank from the US. What've you got to say for yourself, young man?"

Hank limped determinedly to the spot in front of the chocolate fountain. "Firstly I'd like to thank those who supported 'Bid For A Kid', now enabling vital and urgent things to happen for the planet. Please keep supporting."

The presenter looked taken aback by how much Hank had grown up in just a few days. "Er...so how was the run?"

"Toughest thing ever...but also the best."

"And what do you intend to spend the loot on?"

"I'm setting up a company to defend the rights of the Earth – making sure the laws are changed so that businesses that harm the natural world will be prosecuted. Our ancestors suffered for it. Now I will fight for it. And I know people will listen to schoolkids."

The presenter whacked his face as though checking he was 'with it'. "Well, folks, we'd better watch our step, had we not?... And next we have...?"

He looked over to see...

...The girl who came painfully over on crutches, with only one leg, her stump bandaged up, her afro hair dramatically unkempt.

"So what about you, little Bibi from South Africa? Looks like it's been tough..."

Though her body was a wreck, her dark eyes were burning with a fierce fire. She looked straight at the camera. "I've learnt how amazing it is to have friends and be part of, like, a tribe. I'll never forget this experience."

She shifted her crutches to get comfortable, "I'm going to start a charity to care for the disadvantaged. I'm going to drive a movement."

The presenter was momentarily distracted by the movement of mosquitos...

So Bibi continued, "I want absolutely everyone on the planet to feel part of the whole and not left out, however different they are...even if they see dragons! Then, they'll really want to help the natural world. I know we can do this."

She nearly fell down but allowed the Kahuna to help her back to a seat, where she rested her head on the old woman's shoulder.

By now the presenter was dancing around swiping at unseen enemies. "Viewers, you can see it's been quite a struggle for these kids... I myself can vouch for how altitude brings stuff up – ha ha. Let's speak with our next contestant, who is..." his red blotchy nose went a little pale, "from Russia."

Victa marched over with the strange stiff-legged gait of muscles not doing as requested.

The presenter took a cautionary step backwards. "So, Victa, how was it for you?"

Victa went to start a fighting movement with her hands pointing at the presenter, "I always was strong, but mountain has given me new strength…" She glared forcefully into his eyes.

He looked away and took another step backwards, pleased he'd worn his smart sunhat as he was feeling particularly hot – no doubt the anxiety of his work – but thinking of the viewers, as always, he continued, "And what will you do with your share?"

Victa's legs twitched ominously and the presenter uneasily took yet another step back, as she said, "I'll be bodyguard for polar bear, iconic symbol of Natural World Crisis losing ice home, but also for all animals. I insist vast areas of planet be conserved for them… And use life-force practice to bond with them and hear what they say, so they can show people new ways for all species to live in world together."

"Well folks, somebody'd better warn the polar bears…" The presenter heaved a sigh of relief. He'd survived the Russian attack. But just then he noticed that it was raining…er…he licked his lips… It appeared to be raining chocolate. His hat must have caught the edge of the fountain, diverting a moat of melted chocolate into the rim. He certainly couldn't take his hat off without his hairpiece on… So, bravely onwards…

His voice wavered a little with, "Next contestant please!"

Moz jiggled over, loosening stiff muscles, a slight smile on his face as he saw the presenter's hat.

"Folks, it's our East African from Somaliland. So Moz, what would you like to tell us?"

"On the mountain I learnt about friendship..." He looked down, embarrassed...

"Yes?"

"And this got me to see that I can feed not just my town but poor people across the whole world. A world with no one hungry."

"How's that?"

"In our region we have space in the desert and unlimited sunshine for energy to take the salt out of sea water. So, unlimited clean water to grow food... Among trees in a way that helps the natural world."

Moz hurried away to join the kids.

"Wonderful – a world overflowing with food." The presenter brushed away some of the chocolate rain which was restricting his vision. "And next we have...?"

Josee wandered over, stroking something in her arms.

"Ah here comes sweet Josee from Colombia. Our South American representative. Tell us your ideas, dear."

"The run confirmed for me the importance of working together for the good of all," said Josee firmly. "So we have to put the money to good use... I'm going to reforest the Amazon and include growing plastic-eating mushrooms in my village. We won't have rules. It'll all be run on love principles. Then people will want to be part of it."

The presenter moved in to say something, but then his eyes widened. He had spotted what was in Josee's arms.

Before he had time to move, the hostel cat jumped with an impressive flying leap onto his hat and clung on, having a lovely time licking the chocolate moat.

There was a moment's stunned silence. So the cameraman zoomed in on the happy cat.

"The Natural World Crisis is definitely upon us, folks," the presenter at last spoke, stretching up and trying to extract the cat from the hat without removing the hat from his head. Unfortunately the cat was by now feeling a little insecure and dug his claws into not only the straw, but also the head underneath, with catastrophic results. The presenter suddenly found his arms full of hat and yowling cat all nicely mixed up with melted chocolate.

The cameraman was so fascinated that he forgot to zoom out and viewers had a moment to study a bald head with a lovely scratch oozing blood, now being inspected by interested mosquitos, who couldn't believe their luck.

"Is it my turn yet?" said Tane, going up to replace Josee with a big smile on his face. The interviews were proving not quite so boring after all.

"Yes, yes of course... Now we have Tane from the Pacific islands of Kiribati." The presenter looked down into his arms, unsure what to do, but sure his ratings would go up if he looked like an animal lover. "Nice Kitty.." he murmured. The hostel cat looked up into the big nose of the big-nosed presenter, unsure what to do, but sure he'd get more chocolate to lick if he stayed where he was.

"Er...um...so, Tane, tell us what effect the race had on you." As if he didn't have enough to think about, he was also worried about what this boy might do to the oil refineries...

"I had trouble with painful feet all the way, but discovered that it's possible to push through pain to reach a goal," said Tane, passionately. "So I'm excited that I'm going to take the world's energy tech into the future...using the unlimited power of the sea... Working with the big companies on sea-level rise, with as yet unimagined research..."

The presenter was relieved, and relaxed a little, allowing himself to tickle the hostel cat's tummy. This brought on full-scale kangaroo kicking with hind legs, claws out like daggers.

"Next!" said the presenter, with a slightly higher voice than usual.

Wilga came onto camera, muscles so stiff she was waddling, a bit like the tortoise she'd represented. "Ah, our Aboriginal girl from

Australia. What have you got to say for yourself, honeybun?"

"I learnt that it's okay to do things my own way...and be accepted for who I am."

"That's lovely, dear." The presenter's face was such a grimace of torture that the cameraman thought it would make the programme more interesting to focus in on it.

"So I'm going to get messages from all the native peoples across the world and make sure everyone hears them... I will be the voice for indigenous wisdom, so humans can live in balance with the Earth."

At this point there was a stifled scream as the hostel cat decided this was the moment to claw and scratch himself away from stardom, and catapult off into the bushes, dragging the chocolate-soaked straw hat with him. The camera managed to catch the presenter's look of pain, then utter relief, followed by dismay at the disappearance of the remains of his favourite hat. And, "Always respect the native animals, folks."

The good thing was that for a while it had completely taken his mind off the mosquitos...

Sighing heavily, he dragged his hand over his bald head, inadvertently mixing up chocolate and even more blood, before turning to Choekyi, who was now quietly waiting.

"Ah, here we have Chockice from Tibet in the

Himalayas, our Asian representative. How was it for you, young fellow?"

Choekyi spoke gently. "All interconnected on mountain, so good to wait for everyone on higher path." He stood silently, allowing the flow of the moment to speak.

"Yes?" said the presenter impatiently.

"Spoke with Great Grandfather," Choekyi said, looking at Hank, who looked down, embarrassed. "He, native Hawaiian, say spirit of aloha is to love invaders." There was another silence.

"Are you saying that if you don't like something someone does to you then you give them love?" asked the presenter incredulously. "Don't think viewers are going to go for that..."

"Great Grandfather say powerful healing," said Choekyi, nodding. Then continued, "So with money, will build monasteries for invaders to study. And will help them open hearts with compassion – compassion for all life."

"I see," said the presenter thoughtfully, using his hand to swipe little invaders off both sides of his nose, followed by both cheeks. This created an interesting chocolate and blood war-paint effect that any make-up artist would be proud of.

By the time Lana had hobbled into place, his itching and scratching had begun, which did slightly spoil the artwork. But not Lana's enjoyment of it.

"So, here we have our lovely Lana from Ireland,"

he said. "Tell our viewers what you're going to spend the money on."

Lana couldn't look at the presenter without giggling, so, pushing her plaits back, she turned to the camera and smiled sweetly. "The nature fairies on the mountain told me there will be a happy future with all beings dancing together. They explained that unkindness in the world will stop when humans stop the unkindness within their thoughts. That idea kept me going on the run. I think they got it from the dolphins. I'm sure there's conspiracy among the natural world to bring this about."

"I'm sure you're right," said the presenter, ignoring his own unkind thoughts about insects.

"So I'm going to start a peace school to help people with the wars in their minds to find positive loving thoughts."

"Perfect! Thank you." The presenter scratched madly, certainly wishing he could find some peace from the itching.

She finished with, "I blame Kai. He's the one who got us all to stand tall and see beyond ourselves."

It was Kai's time to come on. He'd been hanging back until last, hoping he'd know by then what he was going to say.

"Folks, it's our dolphin boy from England. Hello Kai. What's your story?"

Kai looked into the camera blankly. And said nothing. There was silence… Then suddenly he felt filled with the love he'd experienced on the mountain. So began, "No, it's the dolphins that are to blame. But Lana's right… I learnt the natural world is there for us if we can only find ways to listen and work with it." He paused. In his mind he saw two cheeky dolphin eyes looking at him above a big wellyboot smile. "So… I'll start a school of dolphin wisdom studies to help people move into the golden era." He stopped speaking, sure there was something else important…

"Thank you Kai… And to all our kids," the presenter said, swiping at a bare patch of forearm which needed painting…

"Well, viewers, I'll end on a personal note… Er, this is embarrassing… I wasn't ever listened to as a child, so my dream has always been to draw attention to myself so I can be heard… But since listening to the visions of these kids I've seen something more important…"

The only important thing to the kids at this moment was that he stop talking so they could get at the food.

But he continued, "They're rising up to save the planet…and inviting the kids of the world to join them… So, all you kids out there…listen up!… You are the voices for your own future."

He turned to the kids, who were slowly

advancing on the chocolate fountain. "You have important stuff to tell the world. I intend to dedicate my life to following you and sending it out."

There were groans of, "No! no! Please! We don't need that!"

"No really, it's nothing... So expect to see a lot of me..."

"No...!"

He turned back to the camera. "So, folks, what I've seen is that...in spite of catastrophic happenings...if we work together for the good of everyone, then each person cares. Then we solve all the problems.

Isn't that awesome?

These kids are showing us we have a golden future ahead. And we'll be working in harmony with the natural world."

As if on cue, out of nowhere came a deluge of rain. The hostel cat belted for cover, straight through the presenter's legs, tripping him up. The last image viewers saw was a chocolate and blood-coloured man rolling on the ground, surrounded by dancing mosquitos.

There were cries of, "Eat, now!"

No problem there.

A little later, when the boys were getting ready for bed and laughing about the evening as good friends do, Kai's phone rang.

"Hi lad."

"Oh, hi Dad."

"Mum an' I watched you on TV... We're proud of you, lad. We've applied for the operation an' that looks 'opeful. Mum says to say, 'well done for standin' tall'... An' she loves you. But there's somefin' I wanna ask..."

"Yes Dad?"

"Was wondering if when you get back...you an' me could go surfin'...like...just you an' me... like...spendin' time together?"

"Okay Dad... That'd be good."

He snuggled up with Phinny to go to sleep, strangely contented.

"We're here now! Be ready for surfin' adventure..."

Kai and Phinn are spy-hopping in their favourite place; boy and dolphin hanging out on a peaceful blue sea, waves rising to tumble near a sandy beach with palm fronds drifting in a warm breeze... Happiness.

"Kai."

"Yeah, Phinn?"

"You know this story?"

"What story?"

"Turnin' turtles! The story of you dreaming me...and you running the race in Hawaii... and all the kids rising up to save life on the planet..."

"Yeah..."

"It's all a dream, you know."

"What d'you mean?"

"Dumpin' dogfish! The whole story's been dreamt by the Snow Dolphin."

"Really? But why?"

"It's her heart-song. Based on the promise the dolphins made long ago to the ancients that they would hold knowledge until the time is right. Then they would call up the prophecy of the boy who will catapult the planet into a new era of peace."

"And that time is now?"

"Yup! She says humans have started chucking out greed and taking on more loving ways of doing things."

"Like on the mountain."

"Exactly. She wants the knowledge to help young humans rise up to show respect for the natural world. To remind the adult humans that they'll do anything for their young – just like the animals."

"But humans are part of the natural world. Right?"

"Of course."

"My granny used to say, 'We're all made of star dust.' I'm beginning to see what she meant now."

"Turnin' turtles! That should be, 'We're all made of sea star dust'. We can't help being connected to every plant and animal like one big family pod."

"Cool!"

"But your granny's right. You've only to look at the view of Earth from outer space to understand that."

"When have you seen the Earth from outer space, Phinn?" Kai scoffs.

Phinn splashes wildly and grins, "Hmm...let me see... Think it must have been Wednesday last week..."

Kai tries to shove him, but he's too quick.

Suddenly the sea is alive with splashes and sparkling light. And brother and sister dolphins are all around, diving and spinning and flying. There's an erupting sense of pure joy.

Then an enormous flash of light and the beautiful Snow Dolphin appears in front of them, wise eyes shining with love, spy-hopping as gleaming white flippers momentarily come together in front of her. "Thank you for believing, Young Human. The dream is our call to action."

She turns and dives, lifts her great tail and whacks

it down powerfully.

Kerploosh!

Kai feels the whoosh strongly up and down his back.

It's the call to action!

He feels it with every part of his being – not only with his dream body but throughout his entire physical body too.

Then she is gone. Along with the brother and sister dolphins.

And he can still hear the tinkling music of her parting words, "Please send it out into the world."

Kai is left thoughtful.

Phinn jumps high and schwashes him with a huge bellyflop. "C'mon, let's go and dive for pebbles..."

Kai laughs, "Actually Phinn, I gotta go..."

"Go? Why?... I thought everything was supercool."

"It is...but I've just realised there's something important in my world I must do. You might like to help..."

"Dumpin' dogfish! What is it?"

"Well, you know you said it's possible to do natural magic by concentrating hard and visualising an outcome?"

"Yup."

"And it'll sneak stuff out of the dream and into the physical world, turning things golden – the best that they can be."

"Yup..."
"That's what I'm going to do."
"With what?"
"A book. I'm going to write a book..."

Farewell from the Snow Dolphin

Dear Reader,

You have just read that precious book.

The Young Human gave me the words and I gave them to the author, Tess, who promised to pass them on to you...

This means that I, the last of the snow dolphins, have now fulfilled the task.

So please, listen well on your Sonar.

And keep passing on the dolphin magic, ...peace messages in the ocean of time...

Thank you.

THE SNOW DOLPHIN

'When human thoughts become
peaceful, then violence
on Earth will stop'

'Working together with love
for the good of everything'

‘Courage to connect with things,
not be against them’

'Ho'oponopono
– I'm sorry, please forgive me,
thank you, I love you'

Twelve-year-old Torma takes on a quest to find the heart of a country and a lost penguin. Along the way, it also becomes a vital secret mission to protect the planet from Shady Forces. She hikes across Nepal into Tibet – now full of dangerous Invaders. But she is being hunted. And she is all alone. Help is at hand from her best friend, who is a voice in her head. But can he be trusted?

ISBN: 9781785632075

Yannick, the soft-toy penguin who accompanies Tess Burrows on all her extreme adventures, tells us about them from his particular perspective. He has absorbed some of the teachings that have inspired Tess herself, and his own inner journey unfolds during his extensive travels with Tess. In his simple way, Yannick reminds us of the things that matter most.

ISBN: 9781785630170

We share in Tess' experience of the vibrancy and colour of Africa as the gutsy and compassionate grandmother takes on Kilimanjaro, the highest mountain on the continent. For this peace climb, as a metaphor for people pulling together, she drags with her a tyre filled with peace messages, but can she make it to the top of a mountain that defeats sixty per cent of those who attempt it?

ISBN: 9781903070895

Tess Burrows sets off on a spiritual mountaineering mission to climb to the highest place on Earth – 2,000 metres higher than Everest – to broadcast thousands of peace messages in support of the Tibetan people. No one expects it to be easy, but the extreme challenge to both body and mind pushes Tess towards the ultimate point within herself as she nears the ultimate point on Earth, relative to the planetary core.

ISBN: 9781785631153

Old-age pensioners Tess and Pete journey across the coldest, driest, windiest place on Earth, with the intent of reaching the South Pole to read out peace messages collected from people from around the world. Their mission was to promote peace on Earth, and Tess charts their highs and lows as they haul themselves and their kit across the Antarctic continent in pursuit of it.

ISBN: 9781903070789

Author's Tale

Over the past twenty-five years Tess has worked for the Earth; as a peace campaigner, an extreme adventurer and a wise granny of six! She has sent off thousands of individual messages, many written by children, from the far high points of the planet, in the Tibetan tradition of flying prayer-flags to bring peace and harmony. This has created a six-pointed star of peace – North Pole, South Pole, Himalayas, Andes, Pacific and Africa, raising over £180,000 for charity.

When running up the world's tallest mountain in Hawaii on the Pacific Peace Climb, she asked the dolphins in a native ceremony to take the essence of the peace messages to the part of the mountain below the ocean. After this, she found herself automatically writing information from the dolphins. She made a promise that she would speak for them. This story, *Call of the Snow Dolphin*, is honouring that promise.

The achievement and courage of the kids in the story was inspired by that of the author's thirteen-year-old granddaughter Elsie! Together granny and granddaughter, with their friend Rima, cycled 600 miles to Glasgow's COP26 for climate change. The gruelling journey took them three weeks, carrying camping kit to sleep in hedges and haystacks, and speaking at schools along the way.

At COP26, Elsie presented climate action pledges to world leaders. And was welcomed as a voice for youth.

Hope for a golden future.

Proceeds from this book go towards helping dolphins supported by climbfortibet.org.
see also tessburrows.org

"If you think you're too small to make a difference, try sleeping with a mosquito..."
THE DALAI LAMA